# Secrets and Sins

## Rosalyn Wraight

*To Mary*

a Don't Waste Daylight publication

# Chapter 1

*April 7th 5:45 PM*

*A cold sweat and a heavy heart mock me as I enter these words tonight. I am fearful to even write them, and yet, I know that I must. Thoughts gnaw away at me; I have picked myself to the bone trying to surmise a way to change things. If I cannot, then let these words speak as proof of the circumstances at hand.*

*It seems my countless thoughts about Alex have conglomerated themselves into a conclusion that confuses me. How foolish I was not to have seen it sooner! How foolish I was not to have fathomed her <u>innocent</u> suggestion that I increase my life insurance, get my affairs in order. Amid our conversation about Mother and Father's deaths, about our own aging, I merely took it as sisterly concern. Certainly not as a deviousness pointing to her preparations to kill me!*

*Are her financial burdens so heavy that she could place a bounty on my head? The ledger shows my many attempts to help her, but obviously she wants more: the lifestyle she was accustomed to before three divorces and lunatic extravagances took their cut.*

*Has she sunk so low in her selfishness and greed that she could reduce her own flesh and blood—her own brother—to the monetary buoyancy of inheritance?*

*My sister. My own sister!*

*God, I beg to call myself paranoid, filled with the inane suppositions of a lonely old man. If only it were that simple—if only it were precisely that way—what I would not give for that! But her hatred of me, there since childhood, seems to have intensified, festered over these past months. And regardless of my contrary desires, I cannot look away—no more—on that my life undoubtedly depends.*

*Perhaps it is misguided, but I have invited her for dinner this evening. If I can summon the courage, I shall confront her with my suspicions and divert her plan: get her to see how deeply I love her, how far I have—and would—bend to help her. If I cannot, then I will be forced to continue living under her thumb, in fear of my own life.*

*But either way, it is <u>imperative</u> that I hide my fear from her.*

*In the event that the course of the evening fails to meet my expectation of resolve, I have hidden a loaded pistol in the living room. In case . . . just in case Alex is even more mentally unstable than I have theorized.*

Suddenly, the expected, yet intrusive chime of the doorbell echoed through the capacious house. Tobias hastily scrawled: *I must go–she is here. God help me.* He placed his pen between the confessionary pages and gently shut his journal. As he rose from his chair, he braced himself against the grand mahogany desk and gasped a breath of desperate fortitude. With lingering reluctance burdening his steps, he withdrew from the study and headed toward the front door.

Alexandra had concluded her third and crescendoing succession of knocks by the time Tobias reached the huge oak door. With a twist of his hand and a mighty creak, the door flared, allowing Alexandra's words to enter before her. "For God's sake, Tobias, what took you so long? You were expecting me—you did invite me."

In her whirlwind manner, she entered the hallway, snagged her trench coat on the coat tree's limb, and shoved her ivory-handled umbrella into the stand. "It's supposed to rain later. I just got my hair done, and I am not about to ruin it in any downpour. Oh, and I brought the bottle of cognac you asked for," she said, impatiently handing him her tote bag. "I suppose there's a reason you had me go to such trouble and expense. You have a reason for everything, Tobias, but regardless, here it is."

"Good evening, Alex," he said, trying to appear unruffled by her usual tempest. He carefully clutched the handles of her tote bag and continued,

"Your hair looks lovely. Oh, and thank you so much for bringing the cognac. Do—do, come in."

Alexandra took an abrupt, almost breakneck turn to peer at him, her eyes squinting tightly in skepticism. "My, you're in an unusually good mood tonight, dear brother. What was there? A sale on fertilizer today?"

Tobias chuckled, but inwardly he grimaced, sensing the inevitable onset of her ridicule. "No," he replied. "But now that you mention it, there is something I must show you. Please, come with me."

Ardently, Tobias strode through the living room, depositing the tote bag on the bar as he passed. He made his way into the dining room, beyond the table that had been so elegantly set for dinner. Then he came to a sudden halt and waited for Alexandra to catch up. Curiosity chased her until she stood before him. Then, Tobias turned to face the door.

"The greenhouse!" she exclaimed, disappointment twisting her face. "I should've figured as much." She shook her head, sarcastically adding, "Boy, this'll do wonders for my hair."

Tobias ignored the nearing of her predestined tirade, clutched the doorknob to the greenhouse, and pulled it open. A warm draft of tropical air escaped, the humidity dabbing their faces as they entered. With a gentle snap, the door quickly closed behind them, hoarding the essentials of survival.

The hothouse ran an incredible distance, nearly the entire length of the large house. In Tobias' mind, it stretched eternally—when compared to the small back room he had started with many decades before: hobbyist turned amateur turned fanatic.

Three rows of wooden stagings outstretched, and atop each one, vigorously grew his beloved orchids, hundreds and hundreds and hundreds of them: species, tribes, and subtribes—yellows, purples, black, the whitest of whites—commoners and rarities. Some boasted gigantic sprays over three feet long; some modestly hid their beauty, a subterranean existence. Each and every one, in this, his enormous glass house, seemed to flourish under his devoted care. Perhaps because of him. Perhaps for him.

"Orchids are like people, you know," Tobias began, succumbing to the philosophical mindset the greenhouse always gave him. He had begun the thoughts that notoriously entered his mind in this room, his sanctuary. But before he could continue…

"Come, now! You think of them as people, Tobias," Alexandra interrupted. "That has always scared me about you. You spend your entire life with them. Do they keep you warm at night, dear brother?"

"Do you really want to start this, Alex? Can't you just for once show

3

interest in something that gives me pleasure? Can't you just once try to see the world through my eyes?"

"I'm not starting anything," she snapped her defense like a streak of lightning. "I'm in here, aren't I?"

"Fine, then," he concluded and wended his way between the second and third rows. He sliced through the hum of the fluorescent lights and the whirl of the fan, through the hiss of the hot water pipes and the nearly inaudible *drip drip drip* of the humidifier. Soon, he approached a potted orchid that seemed separate from the rest. He stopped and outstretched his hands in a welcoming gesture.

"Alex, do you remember Kim Su?" he asked, his voice carrying an air of reminiscence mingled with a sense of anguished betrayal for daring to give such memories voice.

"Kim who?" Alexandra bellowed, her nose cricked, her ignorance masked by banter.

"Kim Su," he repeated, enunciating each word. "The groundskeeper Mother and Father had when we were children—do you remember him? He lived in the shed out back, slept on the floor, even after Mother offered him the guesthouse. Kim Su," he repeated once more. "Do you remember?"

"Oh, vaguely, I guess," Alexandra offered, waving her hand in a dismissive motion. She busied herself with a sudden and overwhelming curiosity with the things around her. She perched her nose in front of a bluish Vanda, gently ran her finger on the underbelly of a slipper orchid, and marveled at an Ophrys vernixia that resembled a massive bumblebee.

Tobias recognized her feigned interest in his life's work. He wondered if it attempted to hide her failing memory or if she truly lacked even a remote interest in what he was saying. Unsure of the answer, he nonetheless ventured forward.

"Well, I remember Kim Su quite well. Despite how young I was, I learned a great many things from him. But, Alexandra, surely you must remember the day they came to take him."

Alexandra didn't respond. Her attention turned from the greenhouse to her own self. She stretched and smoothed the nylons on her thick legs. She touched her stiffly sprayed blond hair, checking the relative humidity of her vanity. She did everything but look at him with either inquisition or acknowledgment.

Tobias continued, "He escaped Manzanar, the relocation camp in California, during the big riot in '42. He said no one was going to lock him up just because of the slant of his eyes. They were rounding up the Japanese all over in those years, but it meant nothing to me until the day

4

they tracked him down and took him back. It took them two years to find him. He swore he didn't hurt that corporal. Just a few months more and he would have been okay," Tobias said. His eyes seemed almost to glaze over with an ancient pain, his first lesson in losing and letting go. Reticently, he spoke further, "I clung to Mother and cried as they took him. Those bastards! 'Tobias,' he said to me, 'take care of the orchid; it is family.' And then we never saw him again. He was gone."

Alexandra listened distractedly to Tobias as he told his story. Then, he turned and touched the earthen sides of the orchid's pot. "I cared for his orchid as best I could, praying he would be back to claim it. It had been his mother's; I knew how important it was to him. I was certain he would be back to get it. Over sixty years later, I still tend to it, but my own grayed hair knows I will never see Kim Su again."

"You've grown that thing for sixty years?" Alexandra was astounded but appalled by Tobias' adamancy in not letting go. "Don't you think that's a bit much, dear brother?"

"Is it, Alexandra? To keep alive the wishes of a man, to dignify him? To dare remember and foster what he cared for?"

"That's not what I mean. I mean waiting for him."

"Ah, but, Alex, look at it! Look at Kim Su's orchid," he commanded, raising his hand in show.

Alexandra looked but remained dumbfoundedly silent.

"In all the years I have cared for this, it has never bloomed. I have searched high and low for another of its kind, for someone who could tell me the secret of its bloom. There is no one—there is no other plant like this in the entire world—at least, not that I know of. It's one of a kind. Just as Kim Su was. I have an orchid that my research proves to be extinct. Rare orchids go for thousands and thousands of dollars. The pricelessness of this one far exceeds anyone's dreams."

"So, it's expensive. Is that what this big announcement is?"

"No, no, Alex. There are many, many things far more important than money. Kim Su's orchid has finally flowered. That is all. That is the big announcement. It blossomed last week when my watchful eye was closed."

A brilliant orange blossom hailed from a fragile spike like 4th of July fireworks refusing to extinguish in midair. It seemed proud yet sheepish: stared at, exposed.

"My work with these creatures has come full-circle now," he concluded with a mix of triumph and sadness. Then suddenly he exclaimed, "Oh my word, aphids! That will not do." Carefully, he prodded around in the orchid's medium. A small piece of bark fell to the staging, through the slat, and onto the floor.

"Alex, see that cabinet at the end of the row?" He pointed; Alexandra's head followed his finger.

"There's a bottle of pesticide in there. A big green bottle. Would you fetch it for me, please?"

Alexandra seemed disgruntled by his request but obliged him nonetheless. Quickly, she returned, carrying the bottle, and as she handed it to him, he asked, "Would you mind opening it and setting it down? And do be careful."

"Careful?" she asked, searching the label for the expected skull and crossbones. "Perhaps you should do it yourself."

"No, you do it. My warning was more about its smell than its very poisonous nature. It's supposed to smell like an angry skunk, but I really wouldn't know for sure. My nose has never been a good one. A travesty for a flower lover, wouldn't you say?"

Alexandra scowled as she opened the bottle an arm's length away from her wary nose. Cautiously, she set it down beside Tobias' work area.

"Oh my God!" Tobias abruptly shouted, swiftly turning around and nearly knocking Alexandra over in the process. "The duck is still in the oven! Oh, it must be charred. Quickly! I must get to the kitchen quickly."

Tobias dashed out of the greenhouse with Alexandra in close pursuit. When he reached the kitchen, he pulled open the oven door, only to have a smile widen his face. "Looks near-perfection to me," he boasted. "I do hope you are hungry."

After a leisurely dinner, Tobias and Alexandra retired to the living room. Tobias lit a fire in the fireplace, forcing an early spring chill to leave the confines of the house.

"How about that cognac?" he suggested, ramming the fireplace poker into its stand. "Care to do the honors and pour us a glass?"

Alexandra reposed on the beige leather sofa: feet curled under her, red pumps strewn on the floor like hit-and-run victims. Reluctantly, she rose and ambled almost sleepily toward the bar.

"There are two snifters on the top shelf," Tobias instructed as he made his way to the brown recliner. He sat down with the sigh of a long, hard day.

Behind the bar, Alexandra stooped and returned with the snifters. Her long red nails clinked the Austrian crystal like a toastmaster demanding attention. She uncorked the bottle and poured the large snifters half-full.

"This bottle was over a thousand dollars! And the receipt is in my bag, by the way. Why did you insist I went to all the trouble?" she angrily inquired. "The things you expect!"

"This Louis XIII de Rémy Martin is very expensive, but it was Father's favorite," he answered, shaking his head at her ignorance, treating it as blatant disrespect of his memory. "I remember so many times, sitting in this very room, talking with him—watching him rise to pour himself a glass. The more cognac he had, the more talkative he became. But I guess you would not remember such things, Alex. You were always off somewhere, never quite wanting to be a part of the family."

His remark nailed her in place. Motionlessly, she stared at him, a noticeable fire swelling in her eyes until she wallowed in a full-blown glare. She marched toward him, angrily thrusting the snifter in his direction. As he outstretched his hand to retrieve it, she abruptly pulled it away. "You're such a son-of-a-bitch sometimes, Tobias. You understand nothing," she spat, nearly spelling out each word with wrathful contortions of her face.

She again shoved the snifter at him, this time allowing him to take it. She returned to her place on the sofa and stared at him. In extreme discomfort, he looked away, to the teal carpeting butting the white bricks of the fireplace.

Alexandra ranted, "You were afraid to leave their sight, and then you dare condemn me for not being there every minute of every day of every year? Where the hell do you get off?"

Without looking at her, he sheepishly replied, "It's just what I think. It's what I watched you do when we were young, before they died. And now you do it with me. I just wish I mattered more to you."

Alexandra released a burst of air through her nose and shook her head. "Yeah? And what about your disregard of me?" she challenged. "Did it ever occur to you that I have the right to have a life? That being a hermit in this tomb is not my idea of a life?"

"No, three blood-sucking husbands is much better an existence. But I'm good enough when you need money, though, aren't I?"

Tobias suddenly became silent, realizing he had crossed the fine line that stretched between her reason and rage. He winced, fully expecting a verbal bludgeoning to ensue—but the room remained deathly silent. Cautiously, he raised his head and found Alexandra swirling the cognac in her snifter. She painstakingly twirled the glass, making the amber rise dangerously close to the brim. She stopped and swilled a mouthful, and then her eyes returned to him.

"Is that what this is all about? Your blessed money?" she asked.

"This has nothing to do with money," he defended, drawing enough courage to look her directly in the eyes. "I'd give you all I have. You are my sister, and despite your belief to the contrary, family is of the greatest importance to me."

"Yes, sure, Tobias. Is that why you contested Mother's will? You tried to get it all for yourself and leave me in the lurch. That's how important family is to you. That's how willing you are to give it all away."

"That's not true. You were having problems with Dominic then. You said he was cheating on you and taking you for all you had. All I did was try to tie it up in court long enough for you to divorce him. And as soon as you did, did I contest it anymore?"

"You didn't contest it because you knew you were about to lose."

"That is not true."

Alexandra looked away from him—unconvinced, sickened perhaps.

Tobias took a hefty drink of his cognac and leaned his head onto the back of his chair. His eyes pierced the high ceiling with forceful and racing thoughts. He took a deep breath and moved to a perfectly straightened stance. He looked at her. "Why have you always hated me, Alex?" he posed his lofty question. "I have tried all my life to figure it out. Did I do something? Did I not do something? I can handle the truth. I want the truth. Why have you always hated me?"

Alexandra leaned forward and held her face in her hands. She remained quiet for what seemed an eternity to Tobias. Finally, she assembled her answer and began, "You are so spineless. Exactly as Mother and Father wanted you. They could mold you into exactly what they wanted. A little replica of themselves, a little token to show the world. That is why they loved you more than me. They hated me for what I stood for. I just wanted a life. I wanted somebody to love me without goddamn strings connected to it all." Tears spiraled in her throat; she swallowed hard and continued, "You talk about giving me money, but you do nothing to loosen the strings you attach, dear brother. Instead, you try to tie them into a noose to hang me with."

"There are no strings!" Quickly, he reached into the drawer of the end table next to him. He wielded his ledger at her. "You want it all? I'll write a goddamn check and give it all to you. I don't care about the money!"

"Bullshit!" she snapped. "Spare me your dramatics. You'd die having to leave this house, fend for yourself, actually make a living, instead of leeching off them. Even dead, they still have you dependent on them. And yes, I'm drowning in debt, and you offer to help. But not without the same kinds of strings they attached. Live your life this way, Alex. Don't love that man, Alex. Your dress is too short, Alex. Get rid of that bastard, Alex. Come live at home, Alex. You try to buy me. Perhaps you should find yourself a woman besides your sister, Tobias."

At the last breath of her remark, Tobias flung the ledger forcefully toward her. It hit the arm of the sofa and slide to the floor, spine-up and twisted. He swiftly rose from his chair, charged, and stood within inches of her. She peered fearlessly up at him as he towered above her. Violently, he grabbed her and then retreated.

"There's a gun in the drawer there," he said, pointing with his head as he returned to his chair. "Go ahead and kill me. If I am so deplorable to you, just go ahead. I really don't care anymore."

Alexandra's eyes were wide and calculating, but she did not move. Instead, she held her forearm, soothing the scratches Tobias had left on her with his grasp. She grabbed a tissue from her pocket to dab at the pooling blood. She spat, "You are crazy, Tobias. If I wanted your money, I'd find a better way than that. Perhaps I should just start documenting your insane outbursts—like this one—and have you declared legally incompetent. That would be a kicker, hey, dear brother?"

She laughed maniacally at him, boasting the upper hand she had always managed to have against him. She walked toward the dining room, chanting under her breath, "Such a stupid little man. Such a little, little man…"

# Chapter 2

"What we got, Jansen?" McCallister asked as she rounded the rear of her blue car, removed her sunglasses, and slid them into the breast pocket of her bomber jacket. "I hadn't even made it to the station when I got the call. Now, Jansen," she stressed, sternly thrusting her finger at him, "I start my vacation tomorrow afternoon. I won't tolerate any screw-ups or delays."

Jansen, who had been vigilantly awaiting McCallister's arrival, moved apprehensively from the curb and headed up the sidewalk with her. He recognized she was in no mood to be impeded, but then again, he reminded himself, she never was. Investigations always fevered her—vacation or not.

He flipped open his notebook and began to recite the details of the crime scene. "Man named Tobias Faraday, seventy-three, found dead this morning by his housekeeper."

"Always the damn housekeeper, huh, Jansen?" McCallister chided as she slipped under the yellow police line and climbed the front step of the huge house. She turned to scan the neighborhood. It, she suspected, maintained an air of quietude when not marred with police cars, a coroner's van, and the local media. "So what else, Jansen?"

"Housekeeper said the front door was ajar when she arrived at eight," Jansen continued. "Said she entered the residence and found Faraday on the floor in the living room. Said she didn't touch anything but the telephone. I have her out back; Jessop is questioning her."

Surveying the mayhem around her, McCallister seized mental photographs of the people who had come to watch. A small group gathered along the police line, butting the sidewalk. The usual ghouls, she surmised. In the distance, she spied a woman, clad in a housecoat and curlers, pulling weeds from a flowerbed: a pitiable attempt to portray apathy. A stout man stood motionless on the corner, mindlessly gripping a leash; an impatient basset hound tugged and pleaded for the relief of an elm, only feet away. A mail carrier lingered on her rounds; her hat tipped to block the sunshine that tried desperately to burn off last night's rain.

From her vantage point, McCallister suddenly felt as if she loomed far above the neighborhood and its people. The high step seemed a pulpit from where she preached the presence of the law: its watchful, protective eye—now its suspecting eye.

Abruptly, she turned and entered the house. In the foyer, she slipped booties over her shoes and a cap over her dark blond hair.

"This way, Detective," Jansen respectfully directed, guiding her through the entryway and into the living room. As she followed, she stretched gloves over each of her hands. The snap of the latex arrived in the room before her.

"Morning, Laura," Peter Hastings, the medical examiner, greeted her, only briefly raising his head. Diligently, he continued his work as she neared and crouched next to him.

McCallister's eyes dutifully fell to Tobias Faraday. His rumpled body lay face down in front of the fireplace: a marionette with severed strings; a thing to be bagged and tagged like a sirloin from the butcher shop; a DB; a corpse… There were a hundred names for it, a hundred descriptions: a synonymy. McCallister quipped them all, doggedly awaiting the day when a cadaver did not chill her bone.

"This really a job for Homicide, Hastings?" McCallister asked. "A dead old man … no doubt natural causes. Maine is so beautiful this time of year," she added, knowing full well, by the condition of the room, that a man had not simply expired in some peaceful scenario, reaching the timely and natural end of his life. The set of fireplace tools had been toppled; a couch cushion slumped far from its rightful place; a lamp and a book lay on the floor: mute but reliable witnesses.

"Well," Hastings began, "do you smell that? I mean … other than vomit and urine." His eyes widened, a wordless admission that he asked the near impossible of her.

In eager, yet disgusted assent, her eyebrows knitted together, and she drew the room's scent into her nostrils.

"Poison, I'd say," he announced. "Same smell in the snifter on the table there," he added with a nod of his head. "I'll run a tox as soon as I get him to the lab."

McCallister's heedful eye glanced to the snifter on the end table while her inquisitiveness searched for possible mates. She snapped her finger at a woman entering the room and pointed to the glass on the coffee table. "Lovely shade of lipstick, don't you think, Ristow?"

Ristow rolled her eyes at McCallister as she approached and zipped her windbreaker with the big CSU embroidered on the back. She knelt in front of the table to gather the evidence.

"Okay, so maybe it's not so cut and dry, Hastings," McCallister facetiously confessed, turning abruptly to face him. "Two glasses, one DB, and a God awful smell. I guess it beats killing time in Robbery. I don't suppose you have any interest in two tickets to Maine."

Hastings laughed. "Laura, you're most certainly the next DB." He jotted notes on his clipboard and added, "Because Holly's going to kill you."

"Yeah, yeah, yeah," McCallister spouted, dismissing the notion with a shake of her head. "Now, let's get on with it. Are you going to roll him or what?"

"I was waiting for you." Hastings proceeded to gently turned the body to a face-up position.

A ghastly expression remained on the elderly man's face, non-gatherable evidence of the trauma that had stifled his existence. The left side of his face was purple, and vomit edged his gaping mouth. His eyes were widened, nearly beyond their sockets, allowing the cloudy gaze of death to peer into McCallister.

"Jesus, close the poor man's eyes, Peter," she directed, forcefully breaking her stare. She looked to Hastings instead, and then she further scrutinized the room. "How long, you figure?"

Before a response had even formed in Hastings' mind, McCallister moved away. She withdrew a pen from her pocket and carefully opened the drawer of the end table directly in front of the body. Both he and McCallister spied the handgun in the drawer.

"I wonder if he was reaching for that. Obviously, not soon enough," Hastings remarked.

McCallister proceeded to the bar, purposefully allowing Hastings the time he needed to complete the tasks that would give him an idea about time of death—necessary tasks that she detested watching. In her search of the bar area, she spied a smeared, barely legible liquor store receipt, an empty tote bag, a trench coat draped over a stool, and a half-drained bottle of cognac. As she stooped to investigate the shelves' contents, she noticed an ivory-handled umbrella leaning against the side of the bar.

"Laura," Hastings called to her when he finished. "I've got a core of 88.2, but that was most likely slowed by his proximity to the fireplace. Livor is set. Rigors isn't full, but it's awfully close. I'd say he's been dead eight to ten hours, but keep in mind that if it was poison that killed him, it probably wasn't immediate."

She stopped what she was doing and stared intently at Hastings. Then she pulled up her sleeve to look at her watch. "Between ten and midnight, then," she clarified.

"That would be my guess at this early stage," Hastings said.

"All right, guys," she yelled to get everyone's attention. "Jansen, I need a quick—" Before she could finish her directive, Jansen approached and handed her a notebook page with a rudimentary sketch of the house's layout. She smiled at her own predictability and his efficiency. She quickly studied the drawing and then said, "Cruz and Jansen, you two take the bathroom, study, and kitchen. Bartholomew, you take the upstairs. Jessop's got the outside. I'll do the sitting room, dining room, and greenhouse. Ristow, finish your business in here and then stick with me. You all know your stuff, so do it. And people…" She paused and glanced at each one individually. "Mr. Faraday needs our help, but please, *please* keep thinking about how beautiful Maine is this time of year." She smiled briefly and then spun on her heels.

Eagerly, she began her tasks in the front sitting room. It was a dimly lit space, even with the sun filtering in through the blinds and making intense strips on the room-size Oriental rug. Nothing seemed out of place; in fact, it was immaculate. An eclectic mix of oil paintings hung on the wall, each with an idle picture light clamped to the top.

Finding nothing of concern, she headed toward the door, but suddenly out of the corner of her eye, she spotted something that caused her to stop dead in her tracks. The last painting on the wall sported a tugging familiarity. She leaned closer to the painting of a flower to check the signature, and there she saw "Holly Crawford" in all its loopy glory. Her lover of ten years had painted it, and at first, the knowledge brought a smile to her face. Then a feeling of disgust spiraled from the pit of her stomach to her throat. Holly had sold many paintings, but the idea that one of them now hung at a murder scene made her want to seize it from the wall and run as fast as she could. Instead, she took a deep breath, exhaled slowly, and exited the room.

She headed into the dining room where Ristow now took photos. The table was still laden with remnants of an apparent dinner for two. Studiously, McCallister noted the positions of plates and silverware. She jotted a food items list that would aid Hastings in the autopsy.

Next, she entered the greenhouse through the wide-open door. Her eyes marveled at the incredible span of flowers before her. As she wended her way up the aisles, she acknowledged that each step through the house allowed her to apperceive the life of the Tobias Faraday. Every synonym for the body by the fireplace paled as aspects of his existence, his personality became vivid and clear. The DB became a man.

At the front of the greenhouse, a hodgepodge of pinned notes stuck to an enormous cork board: yellow ones detailed plant names and watering day; corresponding pink ones proclaimed the day for fertilizing. A massive sheet of moisture-damaged paper held taped cards that outlined his entire inventory, citing hundreds and hundreds of plants, each with a specific code. Numerous notes rested on the workbench to remind Faraday to pick up laundry, expect the housekeeper, meet with his broker, set the clocks ahead. McCallister even found one advising him to create a to-do list.

She claimed one more look at what she dubbed his "command center" and continued further into the greenhouse. On the back wall, she carefully opened a cabinet to reveal numerous tools and bottles of pesticides and solutions. Down the third aisle, she found a large, opened green bottle next to space scattered with potting medium. Her nostrils hovered over the bottle, and she easily recognized the odor to which Hastings had referred.

"Ah, the murder weapon," she boasted, rubbing her hands together in delight at the ease of her accomplishment. "Ballistics will have fun with this one." She chuckled, knowing how each specialist got hyped at the prospect of doing the work they loved. The city of Granton hardly afforded many occasions, but when it did, people jumped at the opportunity. Ballistics would be sorely disappointed.

Suddenly, Jansen noisily entered the greenhouse and approached her. "I found this in the study," he began. "Prints were lifted already. I thought you'd want to see it right away."

He handed her a leather-bound journal with the initials "TAF" boldly embossed in gold on the cover. McCallister opened the book to page after page of journal entries, scribed with a meticulous penmanship.

"The last entry, Detective," Jansen eagerly persuaded. "I think it might help you figure this out."

McCallister raised only her eyes to look at him. Her expression censured his self-praising directive, one that insinuated no sleuth of her own. Just as adamantly, her eyes lowered and returned to the pages. "Send Ristow in on your way out, Jansen."

"Yes, Detective."

As he dispiritedly headed toward the door, McCallister quickly scanned the last entry of the journal and yelled to him, "And find out where this sister lives."

McCallister mindfully read: *April 7th 5:45 PM ... A cold sweat and a heavy heart mock me as I enter these words tonight. I am fearful to even write them...*

She finished reading, raised her head, and found Ristow patiently waiting. "The murder weapon is over there," she said with a stab of her index finger. "And do your magic on the rest, Ristow. I trust you know what's important." She left her to her work.

As McCallister made her way out of the greenhouse, she paused at the workbench and quickly compared the journal's handwriting with the slew of notes. Once satisfied, she continued on until the study's doorknob succumbed to the twist of her hand. The sweet scent of good cigars greeted her as she entered.

The room seemed to shimmer as the morning sun streamed in through the windows, bathing the highly varnished woodwork, the paneling, a mahogany desk. Shelf after shelf honored the perfectionistic placement of spines that hailed philosophers, poets, mathematicians, and sleuths. A Michener was surrounded by a Christie and a Poe; Machiavelli cornered Thoreau. All that remained absent from the room's mystique was a great and thoughtful mind to ponder the imagined, to define the unimaginable.

McCallister seated herself in the chair behind the desk and rifled through innumerable papers and notes, pages of an appointment book, and drawers. After jotting down several names, dates, and phone numbers, she returned to the living room.

An impatient Hastings collected the tools of his trade. The body still lay in the cold spot in front of the fireplace, but a sheet had been placed over it—as if sight unseen really changed anything.

"Can I get him to the lab now?" Hastings asked with the whip of frustration sending his words on their way. "You'll get a lot more from me if you'll leave me to my work."

"I understand that, Hastings. I certainly don't want to slow you down, but I need one more thing."

McCallister explained to Hastings that she needed to question the housekeeper and that she wanted to do so in the living room, with the body present. She instructed Jansen to summon the housekeeper as she handed Hastings her list from the dining room.

Soon, the housekeeper arrived, reluctantly entering the room. Her eyes sped reflexively to the body of her employer, and then she quickly turned away.

"I realize this is difficult," McCallister assured, "but I need to ask a few more questions. I'm Detective McCallister. If you'll please have a seat."

"I've answered so many questions, Detective. I would like to just leave and forget this entire morning. I cared for Mr. Faraday. He was a dear man. I cannot believe he is dead—and like this!"

"You'll be out of here in no time. Now, those questions, Miss—" McCallister pointed to a chair near the entryway.

"Mrs. ... Mrs. Jenny Endicott," the young woman corrected as she took the seat. She tugged on her denim dress and crossed her legs. Her hand smoothed her dress, revealing a mid-term pregnancy. Her other hand pulled her shoulder-length blond hair to the center of her back, and then her eyes glanced again to Faraday and back to McCallister.

"Well then, Mrs. Endicott," McCallister began. "You referred to Mr. Faraday as a 'dear man.' I take it you had a good relationship with him. Is that an accurate assessment?"

"He was an eccentric man, but a very dear one at that," Mrs. Endicott explained. "Wouldn't hurt a fly. He was always good to me. Like I told the officer, I've worked for him for three years now."

"And what made him eccentric?"

"He was just such a loner. I don't think he even had any friends. He would see his sister and that was about it. Most of the time he even avoided me when I was here. I would see him watching me from the greenhouse as I cleaned, but he rarely came out to talk to me."

"Tell me about his greenhouse."

"God, he loved those things. He would be in there from the time I got here until the time I left. They're beautiful all right but not if they're all you have."

McCallister inquired about Faraday's countless notes throughout the house.

"He's always been like that, as long as I've known him, anyway. He leaves me a note each week. It always said the same thing—clean this, clean that—but I got a new one every single week. I would even get a note on my check to tell me he was giving me my check. Strange that way, I guess."

"And you always clean on Thursdays?"

"Always."

"Always come in at eight, too, I suppose."

"Well, actually I'm usually here by seven, but this pregnancy is already slowing me down. I called this morning before seven to tell him I would be late. There was no answer. I just figured he was in the greenhouse and couldn't hear the phone. I had no idea that—" Her voice broke, and she seemed to shake her head in disbelief.

"I think that will be all, Mrs. Endicott," McCallister concluded. "If we need anything else, I'm sure Officer Jessop has your address and phone number. Thank you for your time."

The woman slowly rose and exited the house through the front door.

McCallister turned toward Hastings, smiled, and said, "He's all yours, Hastings. Now get a move on! I needed those lab results a week ago."

Hastings smiled at her and shook his head.

McCallister sped to the front door, removed her protective garments,

17

threw them in an evidence bin, and then left to approach the police line that kept the press at bay. In this city, "the press" amounted to three TV news crews and two newspaper reporters. Before she was even within earshot, the who, what, where, when, why and how questions jumped at her.

"I'm sorry, guys. I don't have anything definite, but I swear I'll let you know when I do. Maybe later today," she explained.

The faces before her all drooped in disappointment. She pointed to one of the reporters and asked, "Sutter, can I to talk to you?"

Dirty looks followed the two as they stepped further down the police line in search of privacy.

"Sorry to put you in this position with your colleagues, but I need a big favor, Kate," McCallister said.

Kate Sutter wrote for the *Granton Journal* and had been a close friend of McCallister's for many years.

"Is it the kind of favor that might get me a scoop on your investigation?" Kate asked with a hungry grin. When her question met McCallister's stony, yet smiling face, she reassured, "I was just kidding. What do you need?"

"Holly," McCallister simply said. "Vacation … tomorrow … Holly."

"Oh shit, Laura," Kate declared with widening eyes. "She's going to kill you." She smiled broadly at McCallister. "Can I watch? *Artist Blots Out Detective.* Now *that* would be the scoop of the decade!"

They both started laughing but tried hard to keep it from the watching eyes and cocked ears.

"I know you're probably as busy as me today," McCallister acknowledged. "But if you get a chance, could you stop by our house and see Holly, maybe break it to her before I have to? If she has time to reason it out, she'll hear me a bit better when I talk to her."

Kate smiled and replied, "Sure. It's on my way back to the office. I'll be stuck there all day anyway doing background and waiting for this detective I know to give us some crumbs."

"Thanks, Kate," she said with a smile. "I owe you one."

They began heading back to the glaring group of reporters. Each sported a look that insinuated McCallister had just made Kate privy to the entire investigation. McCallister countered the looks with her own, saying, "All right. All right. It was Mrs. Peacock in the library with the lead pipe."

As she headed back to the house, she enjoyed the discussion among the reporters about how she *always* said that. It was *always* Mrs. Peacock. It was *always* in the library. The weapon was the only variable. One claimed she had even said it at the scene of an accidental pileup on a foggy bridge. If they badgered her, they got blatantly bogus information. They trusted that fact as much as they trusted her when the truth was finally fit for public consumption.

# Chapter 3

McCallister met up with Hastings as he and a tech removed the gurney from the house. Tobias Faraday was leaving home for the last time, and now the press was more concerned with good shots of a body bag than with what any detective could tell them. Priorities were sometimes very pliable things.

She followed the gurney to the van and watched as they shoved it in for its trip to the morgue. Oddly to her, she always felt better inside after the body left the scene. There were no more cloudy eyes that begged for justice. Then it all came down to a one-on-one death match with deception, fighting on behalf of one who was no longer present. She resolutely patted the van's back door after it closed. Somewhere deep inside she made the promise that would charge her with unending determination.

When the van left, she neared Jansen and Jessop, who were going over their notes. Jessop saw her and immediately waved a stout middle-aged man over to them. "This is the next-door neighbor, Douglas Penning," Jessop introduced. He asked the man to tell McCallister what he had observed the night before.

"Like I told the officer," he began, "I was out on my porch in the rain last night about eight-thirty. I was making sure the dog took care of his business and stealing a smoke so the wife didn't know." He paused to clear his throat, almost as a plea not to tell her. "I saw Tobias' sister leave," he continued. "They were arguing pretty loud. She was fuming, but like I said, I don't know what they were saying. The rain was coming down pretty hard. Then she just got in her car and tore off."

McCallister thought for a moment and then asked, "Did you see Faraday at all or just his sister? If you saw him, it's important."

Penning didn't answer right away. He obviously replayed the scene in his mind. "No," he finally acknowledged. "I didn't see him. I heard him, though. At least, I think I did." He twisted his face slowly, as if suddenly doubting himself.

McCallister asked about Faraday's coming and goings, his visitors, his personality. Again, she received a description of a kindly man who was a loner. She thanked him for his help, gave him her card, and asked that he call if he thought of anything else that might help them understand the man and what had happened to him.

Jessop then informed her about a guesthouse on the back property that Faraday rented out. He said he knocked repeatedly, but no one answered. At McCallister's unnecessary suggestion, he agreed to try again throughout the day.

Letting CSU finish processing the scene, McCallister, Jessop, and Jansen agreed to meet a half hour later outside Faraday's sister's residence. Jansen gave her the address, and she returned to her car. For several minutes, she watched the crowd slowly disperse while she made a few additions to her notes. Then, she started the engine and sped off.

Ten minutes later she pulled into a large parking lot beside an old building that looked more like a warehouse than a store. Every liquor and beer advertisement imaginable plastered the large front windows. Where there was a space, a neon light filled it. *Shamu's Liquor:* the biggest sign boasted.

A bell clanged as McCallister opened the door. The passage from brilliant sun to dim light nearly blinded her. As her eyes slowly adjusted, she spied a blond older woman behind the cash register. The woman smiled as McCallister approached. "Can I help you?" she good-naturedly asked.

McCallister smiled in turn, always appreciative of a friendly clerk, one who did not make a patron feel like an imposition. Maybe those 'other kind' only worked in the express lanes at supermarkets.

"My name is McCallister," she stated as she readied her badge for display. "I'm a detective with the Granton Police Department. I was hoping you could answer a few questions for me."

"If I can, I would be happy to."

"Are you the owner?"

"No. That would be Shamu… er… Jim. He's in the back office. Would you like me to call him?" Her face twisted in a way that indicated aversion to the idea.

After declining, she soon discovered that the woman had worked the night before. After indicating that she was aware of the purchase of an expensive bottle of cognac, she said, "I am hoping to get a hold of the credit card receipt if I can."

With that, the slender woman bellowed, "Shamu! I need you up front." She turned to McCallister, informing her that the "boss" would be able to get her what she needed.

22

Soon, a very large man appeared through a curtained door in the back. The loud breaths it took to propel him drowned out the sound of his shuffling feet. His blue-and-white stripped polo shirt barely covered the large, white belly that hung inches over his waistband. His large hairy arms seemed dwarfed and curved against his sides. The words "beached whale" ran through McCallister's mind.

"Yeah?" he asked the cashier, as if utterly inconvenienced by the summons. A wad of skin gathered between his bushy eyebrows as he scowled at her. He was obviously not one of those friendly employees, McCallister noted.

"This detective needs a credit card receipt for a purchase last night."

"Yeah?" he repeated.

"Yeah," the woman fed right back to him with a glare. "It should be an easy one to find. It's not too often when one of those expensive guys comes off the locked shelf."

"Ah, the Rémy," he said, a nearly audible *ka-ching* in his mind when he recalled the sale. "Yeah, I know the one. I'll get it."

As he unhurriedly shuffled off, McCallister browsed the vodka section to kill time. She wondered just how disappointed Holly would be if their vacation had to be postponed. Cosmopolitans always made her bubbly and wild. Then again, Chardonnay brought the philosophical artist to the surface. Then again…

By the time complete indecision had its way with her, the big man returned with the receipt. McCallister quickly studied it, noting the signature of Alexandra Sinclair and the time: 5:17. "I'm going to need to keep this," McCallister informed him. Swiftly, she turned to the cashier and with a wink said, "Thanks so much for your time, ma'am." Behind her, she heard a blast of air from the man she fittingly renamed, "Moby the Dick."

A short time later, she pulled up next to Jansen and Jessop's squad car. Minding the mission, the three of them wordlessly took the elevator to fifth floor of the apartment complex. With a simple knock, came one of those moments McCallister deplored: delivering the news of death.

The door opened only a crack, and McCallister spied a shadowed figure peering out with great reluctance. "Alexandra Sinclair?" she inquired.

"Yes." The answered arrived with a question-mark S.

McCallister quickly retrieved her badge and shoved it in front of the opening. "Mrs. Sinclair, I'm Detective McCallister, Granton Police," she announced. "I'd like to speak with you, please."

"Oh my!" she retorted. "They sent a detective this time! I must be in big trouble. I won't double-park anymore. I promise!"

"Excuse me?" McCallister questioned.

"This is about my parking, isn't it? I only park long enough to get the groceries in," she explained. "I don't understand what the big deal is."

"Ma'am, I think there is a misunderstanding. This is not about your parking. It's about your brother."

The word "brother" brought the door fully open to reveal a sturdy woman who looked much younger and more vibrant than McCallister had expected.

"My brother?" she asked, seemingly shocked. Then, she chuckled at what she apparently deemed an absurdity. "Surely, you jest. Mr. Uppitty would certainly not be in a position that warranted policemen!" She unfurled a roll of laughter in McCallister's direction.

"Mrs. Sinclair, please—" McCallister attempted to interrupt.

"Ah, I know! Dear brother gives to the Benevolent Association," she figured aloud. "Hang on. I'll get my purse." Quickly, she spun around.

"Mrs. Sinclair," McCallister emphatically stated, easing into the doorway behind her. "Please, listen to me!"

Alexandra finally came to an abrupt halt and faced McCallister. A look of suspicion squinted her eyes.

"I'm sorry to have to tell you this, but I'm afraid your brother is dead," McCallister stated very matter-of-factly, knowing there was no pleasant way to say it … to anyone … not even someone with a cloud of suspicion overhead and ready to burst.

"My brother is *what?*" Alexandra demanded. She swiftly put her French-manicured hand to the wall to brace herself.

"Dead, Mrs. Sinclair. His housekeeper found him this morning. I'm very sorry," McCallister said, further entering the woman's home without invitation. "We'd like to ask you a few questions."

"Dead?" Alexandra questioned. She quickly made her way into the living room, unsteadily placing herself on the brown leather sofa. "Why I was just with him last night. What happened?"

"We're not sure at this point. We're doing our best to find out," McCallister assured. "You said you were with him last night. What time did you arrive?"

"Shortly after six. He invited me for dinner." She put her elbows on her knees and flattened her hands to the side of her head. Two diamond rings on thick fingers glinted in the light from the large window.

"And you left at—"

"Before eight, I guess," she answered and then dropped her hands to her lap. "Why are you asking me all these questions?"

"We're just trying to determine the time of death, Mrs. Sinclair," McCallister answered and then quickly continued, "What kind of mood was Mr. Faraday in last night?"

"He was Tobias. What more can I say?" She rolled her eyes, again finding absurdity in the words coming at her.

"I didn't know him like you did. The more information you can give me…"

"I see. I understand," she conceded. "You'll have to forgive me, Detective. This is most upsetting for me. I loved my brother very much."

"I'm sorry for your loss, Mrs. Sinclair, and for all these questions. Now, about last night…"

"Well, he spent most of his time alone. He was not very good at socializing, so it was a quiet evening, and then, of course, he had to complete the evening with one of his tirades." She shook her head and then looked down.

McCallister asked her to explain "tirade" to receive a description of a cantankerous old man who imposed his opinions on everybody. "I think he got that way when he'd been with people too long," she added. "It was almost like he was trying to make them go away. I've always known this about him, so I just left when he got that way. I always accepted him the way he was, moody or not." She smiled at McCallister in a self-appreciating way.

"And what was his tirade about, Mrs. Sinclair?"

"Why his orchids, of course. He could not fathom how one could simply not be impressed by his collection. They're beautiful and all, and his thumb was certainly green, but to spend my time staring at them… Well, he just couldn't understand that—never did."

"So did you argue?" McCallister asked without a tinge of accusation or prior knowledge.

Alexandra paused for a moment. She ran a hand over the nylons on her leg, smoothed the red skirt that hung below the knee, and then returned her eyes to McCallister. "I wouldn't call it an argument," she finally responded. "Just brother-sister stuff." Tears suddenly pooled in her eyes.

"Can we call someone for you, Mrs. Sinclair? Is your husband here?" McCallister asked. "Jansen, go get her a drink of water."

Alexandra shook her head. "I'm alone. I'm fine, though. I'm fine. Actually … I'm all alone now … alone … if my brother is truly gone."

McCallister tilted her head toward Jansen and again asked him to get her a drink of water. He followed her instruction, his eyes dutifully scanning the apartment as he did so.

McCallister returned her attention to Alexandra, who simply stared at the white carpet. She allowed the silence to continue unabated until Jansen returned with a glass. He handed it to Alexandra, and she took a quick sip and placed the glass on the end table.

"So other than that, the evening was uneventful, Mrs. Sinclair?"

Alexandra nodded attentively, and then her eyes glazed over, her focus very distant.

McCallister kept on calmly, "Did anyone arrive while you were there? Did you see anyone when you were leaving?"

Again, Alexandra answered with only a shift of her head. Then, suddenly, she sat straight up and glared at McCallister. "What kind of questions are these? You're making it sound like someone did this to him or something!"

McCallister assured her that they simply needed a complete picture of what had taken place in his home that night before any conclusions could be drawn. She assured her it was all a matter of procedure. She assured her of things that leaned far from the truth. A journal entry … fear of being killed … by this woman … his sister, now sitting in grief, vulnerably, in a room overlooking a rushing river.

She continued, "So, to make sure I've gotten an accurate picture… You arrived shortly after six for an uneventful evening. Mr. Faraday had a tirade because of your lack of interest in his orchids. You left some time before eight. And you witnessed no contact between Mr. Faraday and anyone else. Is that correct, Mrs. Sinclair?"

Alexandra nodded once more. "That is what I am saying, Detective."

"Just a couple more questions, and then we can leave you be. What time did you eat dinner, and what time did you arrive home last night?"

"We ate … probably around six-thirty, and I got home around eight-thirty. I would have paid better attention had I known it would be so important. But, if I had known how important it really was, I never would have left him at all."

"Thank you for your time," McCallister said abruptly and then handed her a card. "My number is on here, if you can think of anything else. I'm not sure when the coroner will be releasing Mr. Faraday's body. I suggest you give him a call. And I would also advise that you remain in the area until we have all the facts, Mrs. Sinclair. We may need further information."

"Oh, I'm not going anywhere, Detective," she snapped. "I have a brother to bury. I'm all he had."

McCallister stood and said, "Oh, I almost forgot. We're going to need to get fingerprints from you, Mrs. Sinclair." She sensed an angry objection coming, so she quickly assured her while motioning Jessop over to get on with it. "No doubt your prints are all over his house, since you two were so close and it is the family home. By getting your prints now, we'll

26

be able to eliminate yours from any others we find. Your prints *should* be there. I don't want anybody questioning them."

"Yes, they should be there, Detective," she affirmed, as if that fact completely absolved her from any wrongdoing, criminal or otherwise.

Once the printing was complete, the three of them dismissed themselves.

Even before the elevator doors closed, Jansen questioned, "Why didn't you haul her in?"

"An officer who jumps the gun. That could be a dangerous thing, don't you think?" she challenged and then turned to Jessop. "I want an unmarked car out here at all times. I want to know *all* her comings and goings until Hastings gets his work done. And her prints needed to be at the lab a week ago."

Jessop nodded emphatically and scrawled in his notebook.

McCallister looked at Jansen's squinting eyes as they left the elevator. "What is it, Jansen?" she asked, making it obvious that she was downing her guard.

"Nothing, Detective."

"Come on, Jansen. Out with it. I know we missed lunch, but I promise not to bite your head off."

"All right," he cautiously began. "I just can't figure out why you're not bringing her in. The journal points the finger right at her. The neighbor saw her come and go … half an hour *after* she says she left. He heard them arguing. It's all right there: motive, means, and opportunity. You insist we go by the book, Detective. This *is* the book!"

"And your guts, Jansen—something that's not in the blessed book. What do your guts tell you?" she pushed.

"She did it, Detective. It's the only thing that makes sense."

"Sense," McCallister repeated. "More information will only give us more sense."

"But she'll get away, hide evidence. That won't bring sense," he boldly defended.

"What is she going to do? Ditch the murder weapon? Wash the blood off her hands? I have a feeling that this one will tell us far more by what she does than by what she says. And I want to know *everything* she does from here on out."

Jansen was still not satisfied. Slowly, he shook his head in frustration. McCallister stared at him, wanting to chuckle at the same time she marveled at his insistence. "Okay, Jansen, haul her ass in then," she dared. "What are you going to get from her when she lawyers up? And then, what are you going to charge her with?"

He knew she was right. His head bowed, but it was not with defeat or feeling censured.

"You hang around me too much," she scolded with a laugh. "You're being impatient when there's no need—not *yet* anyway. Just let Hastings do his thing. There are a lot of things that could have happened other than what it might seem like she did. If she did it, we'll get her. I'll even give you the honor of hauling her in."

"And I'll take it," Jansen said.

# Chapter 4

McCallister eased her car to the curb in front of Timmer's Book 'n Bean. After running in to get a large coffee, she lit a cigarette and pulled the cell phone from her pocket only to stare at it. She figured the sooner she called Holly the better it would be, but she hesitated. It wasn't fear that stalled her. No one who knew them truly believed that Holly would be mad, and yet, a wounded detective was indeed part of the equation. The sense of letting Holly down felt fatal to her, something she would go to great lengths to avoid. But some things in life were unavoidable. She sipped and stared at the phone, suddenly realizing this was one of those unavoidable things. She took a stiff swig of coffee and hit speed dial with tightly held breath.

Before McCallister could even utter a greeting, the consequences of caller ID allowed Holly to spew, "So you're bailing on me, huh? Is that what you're calling for, Detective?" Apparently Kate or the news had filled her in on the city's sudden need for a homicide detective.

"I'm not bailing on you, Hol. Never," McCallister said, her mind trying to gauge the mood. "But I do have to see this through."

"What are the odds, babe? What are the odds?" she bemoaned. "We have a trip planned, a plane to catch, and somebody has to go and whack somebody. I mean really!"

"I know. For God's sakes, I know," McCallister pleaded. "I didn't murder the guy, Hol, and I doubt he was murdered just to ruin our vacation."

"I know. I know." The quick words mixed with a laughter that acknowledged the ridiculousness. "It's just that I was looking forward to this trip, babe. You owe me for that supposed weekend getaway. Christmas shopping in New York—yeah, right! How about hours on end in a cop shop? It was a get-'em not a getaway. When I spend a weekend with the law, I prefer it just be you."

"You're right. I owe you, but I haven't been able to work a murder case since then," McCallister defended. "We moved here from a city where there were murders everyday. I wanted things slower, but I didn't figure I'd miss Homicide this much. It's what I love to do, Holly, and somebody needs to help this poor old man. He can't speak for himself anymore."

"I know. I know," Holly said again, but this time the laughter had gone missing. "Kate told me. I know. It's what you do. It's who you are. I respect that." She paused and then added, "But you have to respect my need to whine about it! It's what I do."

They both laughed, and suddenly all tension slackened.

McCallister teased, "And I want you to know that you're very good at what you do, honey, so you go ahead and whine away."

"Thank you! I will do just that that," Holly said, now roaring with laughter.

"But, Hol, just keep those bags packed. We still might make that plane, or we'll reschedule if we have to. We *will* do it, though. I promise, as soon as I get this wrapped up—"

"I know that, too, babe," Holly interrupted with a confident admission. "I know that. Do what you've got to do. I'm just disappointed, but I certainly don't blame you."

"You don't?" McCallister chided. "Gee, Peter and Kate both predicted I'd be tagged and bagged by the time you got through with me."

"Well, I'm not *through* with you."

"Promise?"

"Just work your magic *fast*, Detective."

A smile cut across McCallister's face. She knew she would work as fast and as diligently as she could, with Holly's desire further charging her determination to find the truth. "I love you, Hol," she said. "I'll be home as soon as I can."

McCallister tossed her cigarette, started the car, and pulled into traffic as her mind rifled through what she knew and what she needed to know. She headed to the station to swap her car for her department-issued one and then made her way back to the Faraday house.

When she arrived, she scanned the area. Just earlier, it swarmed with people. Now, it echoed a quiet that was necessary for her to fully comprehend a crime scene. She parked in the alley behind the house and stealthily made her way to the front door, greeting the officer who stood as sentinel. Assuring him that she'd keep an eye on everything, she relieved him of his post so that he could go have a late lunch. She told him to be back in an hour, figuring that was more than enough time for her prediction to prove itself accurate or not: Alexandra Sinclair would show up.

Making her way to Faraday's study, McCallister listened intently to the stillness. Both the sister and the housekeeper described him as a loner. This quietude, then, was his constant companion, and it knew the truth of what had happened. These walls that had separated him from the world had also protected him—and his secrets.

She sat in the chair behind the grand mahogany desk. He was an intellectual, she surmised, as she gazed upon the innumerable books. He cultivated his mind as much as his prized orchids. Despite the emptiness that others described, he had filled his life and his mind with things that gave it meaning.

In one corner of the room, a wobbly stack of old *Chalkline Mysteries* magazines reached almost to the ceiling. In the opposing corner, *Watson's Enigma* magazines formed an equally formidable tower. These cornerstones seemed as though they were an audible challenge from Faraday—an old man who obviously loved a mystery. Only this time, he was the center of it.

"Is it really as simple as it looks, Mr. Faraday?" McCallister spoke into the silence. "Did your sister do this to you? Your own flesh and blood?" She shook her head, believing there was no form of murder more deplorable than familial.

McCallister retrieved her phone from her pocket and switched it to vibrate rather than ring. She leaned back in the leather chair and propped her feet up on the desk, something she imagined Faraday had done on many occasions in his life, and she waited.

Soon, she heard a sound from the other end of the house, a sound that did not jar her; rather, it reassured.

Tobias' written words, "She is here; I must go," ran through her mind as she quietly made her way to the source. She careened her neck around the corner to see exactly what she expected. Alexandra Sinclair stood there, glancing around the room, a tote bag in one hand, and an umbrella in the other, and a trench coat over her arm.

"Mrs. Sinclair," McCallister challenged, "fancy meeting you here."

Startled, Alexandra's entire body flinched. "Detective, you almost scared me to death. What—"

"I guess you didn't realize that 'Do Not Cross' on that yellow tape outside actually meant 'do not cross.' This is a crime scene."

"You don't understand," she countered. "This is more than a crime scene to me, Detective. This is my brother's home. I need to be here."

"To retrieve your belongings?"

"Oh yes, I forgot these last night, but that's not the only reason I stopped by. I needed to see what happened. Where was it that you found him?"

31

"It's not obvious?"

"Well, now that you mention it," she acknowledged as she glanced to the soiled area in front of the fireplace. "What do you think happened to him, Detective?"

"I think he was murdered."

"I mean how? Was he shot? Was he stabbed? Strangled? Did he suffer?" her voice cracked deeper with each question. Tears streamed through the crevices in her composure.

"Do you really think there is a way to be murdered and not suffer?"

"One can hope—hope that it was fast—hope that it was painless."

"Is that what you hope, Mrs. Sinclair?"

"Yes, I hope it was fast and painless." The words seemed to strike her as odd, and she fidgeted. "That doesn't sound quite right. I mean if he had to die, I hope it was fast. He wasn't one to tolerate pain very well. He was a good man. I do not know what I am going to do without him."

"Did he have any enemies, Mrs. Sinclair?" McCallister asked as she walked to within inches of her.

"If he didn't have friends, I doubt he had enemies," she reasoned. "All he had was me."

McCallister nodded and then asked, "Would you qualify as an enemy?"

Alexandra shot her eyes to McCallister and just glared. "I won't dignify that type of question. I loved him."

McCallister merely returned the burning gaze and said, "Love isn't always an airtight alibi." She paused and then fluidly returned to amiable questioning. "Do you know if he had a will, Mrs. Sinclair? We haven't been able to find one here."

"I suppose he did. He was a stickler for details. Have you spoken with his lawyer? Arlen Dorsey has handled our family's affairs for many years," she informed her. Then she stabbed her index finger in the air. "There's a safe behind the portrait of Father in the sitting room. It's probably in there."

McCallister did not reply; rather, she went to the window and parted the drapes. Her cell phone vibrated in her pocket, but she ignored it. "That was quite a downpour we had last night, wasn't it? Seems a shame to have forgotten your umbrella and coat on such a night. Was it raining when you left here last night?"

"Um." Alexandra stretched her mind to recall. "Yes, it was, Detective."

"But you still forgot your things."

"Like I said, my brother was having one of his tirades—it seems so stupid now. I left in a hurry."

"Oh," McCallister replied and retrieved the phone from her pocket as it made its second demand. "McCallister." She listened and finally replied, "Yes, Jessop, I am well aware. Thanks for calling. I am at the crime scene now."

Then, she returned her attention to Alexandra. "I'm afraid I'll need you to leave your things. Mrs. Sinclair. As I said, this is a crime scene, and we'll need it to remain untouched. Could you please put the things back exactly where you left them last night? We made a horrible mess of things, I'm afraid. If you could please put them where they were when you left last night, I'd be most appreciative. I apologize for our mess."

Alexandra angrily turned on her heels and put the tote on the bar. She stomped to the foyer, slammed the umbrella into the stand, and stuck her coat on the tree hook. Upon her return, she brusquely asked, "You still don't know when I can have my brother's body?"

"No, I'm sorry. I don't know."

"Well, I'll make the arrangements as best I can. I appreciate your trying to find out what happened to my brother, Detective." She suddenly smiled at her, but it was far from genuine. It was cursory.

"Good day, Mrs. Sinclair."

"And you, Detective."

When Alexandra closed the front door behind her, McCallister called Jessop back, asking him to summon someone to open a safe and then to secure the scene. She sped into the sitting room and scanned the walls until she found the portrait of a stern-looking older man. Pausing momentarily, she looked again to Holly's painting on the wall. Then, she carefully pulled on the portrait's frame to find the safe that Alexandra mentioned. Unwilling to wait for its content to be exposed, she checked the list of names she had garnered from Faraday's desk and hastily headed to her car. As soon as Jansen and Jessop arrived, she sped off, in pursuit of one Arlen Dorsey.

Soon, she was parked across the street from the law office of Spaulding & Dorsey. She entered to find a receptionist eager to help. When she asked to speak with Arlen Dorsey, however, she was informed that he had stepped out for a bite to eat, to a deli down the block. Pastrami on rye was no excuse to delay an investigation so she decided to find him.

The deli bustled with activity despite the fact that the lunch hour was long over. She remembered that Alexandra Sinclair had described the lawyer as one who had taken care of "family's affairs for many years." Thus, she approached an older man sitting at a high table in the back.

"Mr. Dorsey?" she queried.

He nodded in mid-bite of his sandwich. She introduced herself and flashed her badge.

"Tobias Faraday is dead, Mr. Dorsey," she said and then waited for the man to swallow and put down his sandwich. "I need to ask you about his will."

Dorsey contorted his face. "What happened? I just saw him last week. He looked good. Oh my, this is terrible."

"We're not sure what happened yet, but I need to know what his will states and whether he recently changed it."

"As a matter of fact that's exactly why I saw him, to have him sign the new will he had me draw up." He went on to explain that Faraday's prior will had left the house, his orchid collection, his stocks, and $600,000 to the Department of Botany at the university. He said the rest was to be given to Alexandra, doled out in yearly installments of $80,000. In his new will, he stipulated that everything go immediately to his sister, no strings attached. Faraday also asked Dorsey to make mention in his will of a five-million-dollar life insurance policy he had with Alexandra named as beneficiary. "I think the thing that made the least sense to me," Dorsey remarked, "was that suddenly he was okay with leaving his beloved orchids to Alex. In my mind, he might as well have requested that they all die with him. Alex's thumb is as green as a lemon, and her disposition just a sour. He said he knew what he was doing, and frankly, I had no reason to doubt that."

McCallister thanked him for his time and said that she would have an officer stop by later with an official request for a copy of the will. She ordered a cup of coffee, and as she waited, she watched Dorsey attempt to return to the consumption of his sandwich. It soon became obvious that his appetite had disappeared; he balled up the sandwich in its white paper wrapper and tossed it in the trashcan before leaving.

Armed with new information and a fresh cup of coffee, McCallister sat in her car thinking. Everything seemed to be bolstering Jansen's contention that the sister did it, but "it" was still not definite. Had he really been poisoned or had he suffered a natural death? Seizure? Heart attack? Something accidental? There was only one person who could answer that. Badgering Hastings proved about as productive as reporters badgering her. Regardless, she grabbed her cell and punched his number.

"How's my favorite coroner?" she asked after he answered.

"Busy," he snapped at her. "I'm trying to get you to Maine. Should I be something other than busy?"

"Friendly would be a good start," she dared. "You've known me your whole life, remember?"

"You're right. I've known you all your life, so odds are good that I'm right to assume you're calling to ask for information you should have had a week ago."

34

She couldn't help it; she laughed. "And I know you, too, which means I can assume you'll get it for me."

"Not if I spend my time on the phone arguing with you. These things take time. You know that."

"Well, just to set the bar for your jumping-to-conclusions mind, I'm not calling to harass you for information … unless of course, you have some." She paused, hoping. When he remained silent, she said, "I'm calling to tell you that Faraday's sister said they ate dinner last night around six-thirty."

"Now that is helpful. Thank you, Laura," he responded, knowing full well that she was hoping to be paid for the information with come sort of crumb. He purposefully paused until he knew her hopes were high, and then he added, "Now go away and leave me to my work."

"Not so fast," she shouted into the phone before he could hang up. "I trust you, Hastings. Please, at least tell me what your guts say. Was he murdered?"

"I don't think it's wise to ask a coroner what guts say. Of all the people you could ask, a coroner just might tell you."

"For shit's sake, you're in a mood." She laughed, and oddly, she felt relieved by his banter. Things had been incredibly difficult for him since Stephen, his lover, died several months prior. In that regard, banter was good. Banter was very good. "Your intuition then, Hastings. Was he murdered, or am I chasing my tail?"

"Unofficially?" he asked, knowing full well that it was; nonetheless, he wanted to hear her say it. When she did, he affirmed, "It wasn't natural."

She thanked him and swore to leave him alone until he completed the autopsy.

As the car's clock readied itself to flash three-thirty, she again drove her car in the direction of the Faraday house. If more luck was on her side, the safe would be open and a trove of answers would be had. That reverie came to a swift end when she spied the look on Jansen's face as he paced the sidewalk in front of the house. She exited her vehicle to be bombarded with, "I swear, Detective. We called right away, but nobody's here yet to open the safe. I called again. They said they were on the way."

Before she could respond, a van skirted the curb and a two-member team swiftly emerged. Jansen bit his tongue and simply pointed to the front door. "And make sure you lift prints first," he called after them.

McCallister smiled. He did hang around her too much. Always yell at someone *before* they make a mistake, not after when it becomes too late.

"What about the guesthouse, Jansen? Any progress there?" she asked.

He shook his head. "Still no one home. I checked, and it's zoned as separate property, so unless we get probable cause for a warrant, we're stuck waiting it out," he said. "The mailbox says 'Thaddeus A. Frederick,' but there's no social or driver's license for him."

When she found out that he hadn't had a chance to check on the residence in the past hour, she volunteered. She started heading around the house but stopped when an idea popped into her head. She quickly headed to the neighbor's house and rang the bell. A grouchy-looking woman answered, and McCallister asked if Douglas Penning was home.

"He sure is," she said, more as a warning than an affirmation. "He's on thirds this week. I'll get him."

Soon he entered the porch with an outstretched hand for her to shake. "Detective, what can I do for you?"

"What can you tell me about Thaddeus Frederick—the guy who lives in the house out back?" she asked.

"Now that one I can answer for sure," he responded. "I have never seen the guy. Odd, huh?"

"Walk with me," McCallister said, and he followed her without hesitation.

When they reached the back alley, she pulled a pack of cigarettes from her pocket and offered him one. With a greedy and sly smirk, he took one. She got one for herself and lit them both. Then, she asked him to explain why not seeing the man was odd.

"The wife's a real nosy one, she is," he began, lowering his voice. "If she hasn't seen someone in the neighborhood, they don't exist. He's been here several years, and the most we've seen is a light on some nights, sometimes a visitor, but I don't think the guy has ever come out. Can't even tell you if he's young or old." He stopped and took a long drag from his cigarette. "People call Faraday a hermit, but him I've seen, talked to, even borrowed things from him."

When McCallister asked about the visitors, he said that he had seen Faraday going in and out and a middle-aged woman he didn't know. They finished their cigarettes in an amiable silence. She thanked him for his time, and he seemed nearly to bless her for the nicotine fix.

To no avail, she knocked on the guesthouse's front door and then headed back, just as Jessop was yelling to her, "They've got the safe open, Detective!"

# Chapter 5

A feeling of rejuvenation overcame McCallister and propelled her feet to Faraday's sitting room. She entered to find a tech taking pictures of the safe's content. Eagerly, she spied over his shoulder. Looking for what, she wasn't exactly sure, but her insides felt as though there would be something as pivotal as a signed confession, a videotape of the murder—something that would snap all the pieces into their correct positions. Something. Yet, if there were something, she knew she hadn't earned it.

With gloved hands, the technician began to pull items from the neatly stacked pile. A small box contained two wedding rings, most likely belonging to Faraday's parents. Next came a stack of stock certificates, all from Faraday Paper, the company responsible for the family's wealth. Next came the will, dated April 1st of the prior week and prepared by Arlen Dorsey. Next came a life insurance certificate, dated the prior month, March 15th. The last item removed was the current issue of *American Orchidist Association Magazine*. And that was it. All there was.

McCallister was speechless, and all eyes shot to her as if expecting a denouement or least an epiphany. When she realized that she had not filled them in on her conversation with Arlen Dorsey—information that rendered the safe's content common and expected—she did so, only to watch disappointment overtake the hopeful facial expressions. The room went completely silent. It was the grand illusion: If something needed a safe, it had to be valuable enough to require such safety. Treasure versus trash, eye of the beholder—clichés ran through her mind.

Only one thing retrieved was unexpected: the magazine. "Why lock up a magazine?" she pondered aloud, although she posed the question more to herself than the others in the room. "I think we've missed something big, guys. I think it's the damn orchids."

They just stared blankly at her. She double-checked the date on the magazine and then ordered, "Bag all this stuff. Then lock the place up tight. Call the captain and ask if we can have someone posted here or if patrols will have to do. Jansen and Jessop, if your shift is over, go home. If not or if you can get him to give you overtime, head to the station and start on the paperwork. I'm going to the university, and I'll try to meet up with you guys by six. Okay?"

They nodded their agreement, and McCallister started walking to her car, punching numbers on her phone as she went.

"Ginny, this is Laura," she said. "I need a big favor."

Ginny Bleeker was a professor of English at the university and had been a friend for years. If anyone knew the go-to's in academia, it was Ginny. McCallister explained that she needed the best botanist on staff. "If you could have them available in the next half hour, I'd appreciate it. … No, not a sudden need to garden. It's official business." When Ginny assured her that she could do as she asked, she thanked her.

Soon, she parked in front of Timmer's Book 'n Bean again. She asked Mr. Timmer if they carried *American Orchidist Association Magazine*. He got her a copy and a large coffee. She managed to pay and exit without having to deflect the usual questions he posed when there was an investigation underway.

As she eased into the driver's seat, her cell phone gave its text message tone. She looked to find "CFBR6," and a smile spontaneously spread across her face. In lover language, that meant: *Chinese food, bedroom, six o'clock*. It was a ritual Holly and McCallister performed on innumerable occasions throughout the years. It had a way of making a tough day easier to contend with, knowing the two of them would be together soon, jamming chopsticks into each other's mouths in the sanctity of their bedroom.

McCallister punched the seven on the keypad and sent the reply. It altered the plan but did not destroy it; she hoped that a smile would find its way to the other end.

Twenty minutes later, she double-parked in front of the university and found Ginny waiting for her by the door.

"Dr. Marty Spangler is the best we've got. He's also department chair," she announced as she gave McCallister a tight hug. "He said he'd meet us in his office."

"I owe you, Ginny. Thanks."

"Well, can I collect that IOU right now?" she asked, grinning from ear to ear, acting very childlike for a woman in her fifties.

A suspicious McCallister stared at her.

"We never get any excitement here. Can I please just sit in?" Ginny begged. "I'll be quiet—won't say a word."

"Oh, you learned how to do that since we last spoke, did you?" McCallister chided. "Fine. You just have to make sure you keep quiet about anything you hear. I mean it. And that includes not even telling Kris." She knew that adding Kris to the mix stressed the importance of it, as the two had been together twenty-four years and shared everything.

She received assurances all the way to Dr. Spangler's office.

After introductions were made, McCallister asked him if he knew Tobias Faraday.

"Everybody knows Tobias! His work with orchids is truly inspiring," he raved. "Actually, I was just over there on Sunday. Did you know he's grown an orchid for over sixty years? He just got it to bloom. It's rare. It's amazing. It's absolutely beautiful. I took pictures of it for him." He beamed.

McCallister knew another one of those deplorable moments had arrived. She took a deep, fortifying breath. "I'm sorry to have to tell you this, Dr. Spangler, but Mr. Faraday was found dead this morning."

His face went ashen. With his right hand, he repeatedly squeezed and pulled his blond bearded chin. His brow hung. Ginny put her hand on his shoulder and gently patted.

"He was a dear friend and mentor," he finally said. "What happened?"

She explained that she was not at liberty to discuss the details, but she assured him that his help was required to get a full understanding of what happened. She showed him the magazine, explaining that for some unknown reason it was locked in the safe with important items and papers.

Spangler knew immediately. "I'm not sure it requires a safe for any other reason than his pride. There's an article in there about his inventory coding system."

"You mean that big area of notes on the greenhouse wall. That's a system?"

"Well, it's certainly not revolutionary or anything, but the man does— did—a lot of cloning and crossing, but at any given moment he always knew which was which, and what its needs were, its age, its parents. And yes, all from that big mess on the wall. I tried to get him interested in a computer database program, but he was adamant that computers should have nothing to do with orchids." He chuckled quietly. "A very stubborn man, but I guess his age and success with his orchids entitled him to that."

"So why the article then?" McCallister asked. "If it wasn't revolutionary or anything, why enough interest for an article?"

"I'm not sure, but most of the veteran orchidists are listened to without question and very well respected. Old school isn't always bad."

McCallister sought clarification, "So you think that's it? Just his pride treasuring an article about his system?"

When he nodded, she conceded. The one odd piece in the safe brought nothing but perhaps a bit of respect for Faraday's command center. She thanked Spangler for his time and offered her condolences. Ginny have him a hug, and they both left his office.

A moment later, Dr. Spangler called after her, "If you need anything more, I will do anything to help. Anything. Please just ask." He approached and gave her a piece of paper with his phone number written on it. Then, he handed her a photograph. "Would you humor me and take this to his house? Just leave it there. It's the picture of his orchid I took Sunday. I never got to show him." His eyes teared, and McCallister promised she would see to it.

At the front door, Ginny said, "You can have your job, Laura. I couldn't deal with telling people news like that. I don't know how you do it. I'll stick with the kids who can't tell a noun from a verb." Ginny gave her another hug and a kiss on the cheek.

McCallister sped off for the station, a cigarette dangling from her lips and her mind racing.

Jansen and Jessop eagerly awaited her arrival. They grinned as she slid into her chair, depositing tired feet on the desktop.

"Lab report, Detective." Jansen announced. "I think you'll be very interested."

She whipped it out of his hand. Indeed, she was interested.

Jansen didn't bother to wait for her to read it. "They got *only her prints* on the bottle of cognac and the green bottle of poison. They also got her prints on the handle to the cabinet in the greenhouse, the knob to the greenhouse itself, the ledger on the floor, and both snifters."

Then Jessop jumped in, "Plus, Mike backed up what Faraday wrote in his journal about giving his sister a lot of money. Mike said the ledger matches what the bank has to say. They will have cancelled checks ready tomorrow."

And then, McCallister jumped in, "And the lawyer backed up Faraday's claim about changing the will and adding an insurance policy."

"Dead to right!" Jansen yelled. "We've got her! When can I haul her ass in, Detective?"

"That could very well be soon, Jansen. Now, we wait for Hastings," she replied, but something gnawed away at her. She was convinced she was missing something right in front of her face. She assured herself that Hastings' report would make the gnawing cease.

The three of them worked on reports. At quarter to seven, they called it a day.

Clutching an overflowing paper bag in one hand and a keychain in the other, McCallister let herself in the front door of her home. The dim light welcomed her, and she breathed the house's familiar scent into her as if it were salvation.

Across the room, a beautiful face smiled at her. Holly sat at the island in the kitchen. She cocked her fingers like a gun, pointed, and commanded, "Set the bag down, Detective … slowly."

McCallister smiled and complied. She deposited the House of Lee bag on the floor, and then she upraised her hands like any good suspect would.

Holly stood and sauntered over to her, her flowing, knee-length green skirt swaying as she did so. She moved within an inch of McCallister's face, ran her tongue along McCallister's lips, and breathily demanded, "Frisk me, po-po!"

McCallister's body shook with silent laughter as she backed up, bent her knees, and attached her hands to Holly's silken calves. In one fluid motion, she swept her hands up her legs, raising her skirt and drawing her intimately close in the process. When her hands inched a little higher, "Oh God" rushed her lips, and she froze. With breath that felt solid to her, she said, "Holly, I'm going to have to start gluing your panties on you in the morning. Seems more times than not, I come home and you don't have any on." She pulled back and gazed into her wild eyes.

Holly kissed her torturously slow. "I don't know what it is, babe," she confessed with another kiss. "As soon as I know you're coming home, it just hurts to have them on." She kissed again. "It aches so bad … I have no choice but to take them off." This time her kiss lingered until it garnered a moan from McCallister. Holly desperately ordered, "Frisk me, copper!"

Hungry kisses instantly superseded the need for food.

Thirty minutes later the two of them could be found on the bed in their candlelit room: stomachs down, feet upraised, elbows propping them up. They sported matching button shirts and the same contented grins. Greedily, they drank wine and used chopsticks to feed each other.

"You didn't eat all day, did you, babe?" Holly asked with a delicate mixture of frustration and concern. "And don't lie to me. I know you. I know how you get when you work one of these damn things."

McCallister swiftly shoved Moo Goo Gai Pan in Holly's mouth and replied, "I'm eating now, so just let it be. Tell me about your day."

"No! I worked all day to get the whining out of my system before you came home, so *you* just let it be."

They laughed and resumed the consumption of food in silence for several minutes. Then Holly said, "I saw you on the news tonight."

"I bet there was a body bag next to me, huh? That's all the press gives a shit about."

Holly ran her hand up and down McCallister's back. "Kate's not like that," she defended. "Her article didn't have the body bag. Just a nice picture of the guy." When asked what the article said, she replied, "Just that he was found dead, who he was, and that the cause of death was unknown."

McCallister remembered the painting on his wall. "Hol, did you recognize him? Did you know him?"

"The Faraday guy? No." Her face twisted in confusion. "Should I?"

"He owns one of your paintings, Hol. I saw it today."

"Oh, that is so sweet!" she gushed. "I knew he had a sweet face. Which one does he have?"

She tried hard to visualize it in her mind. "It was a flower ... or flowers ... or something like that."

"Oh well, *that* sure narrows it down!"

McCallister elbowed her and then tried to describe it as best she could. "Frilly," "deep yellow center," and "bright pink ... light purple" seemed to jog Holly's memory. She finally said, "The guy said it was an orchid ... something with the word 'cattle' in it. Pretty flower, huh? I saw one at the florist. They said they use them for corsages." She smiled and took a bite of crab Rangoon.

"What guy, Holly?" McCallister asked as she rolled and shot to a sitting position. "What guy told you the name of the flower? Faraday?"

"No! I told you I don't know him. The guy..." She paused to remember and to finish chewing. "A guy commissioned me to paint it. He went through the gallery. He sent a picture and a long letter about what he wanted. He paid good, too."

"Do you know who he was? What was his name? Did you meet him? Did he ask for you or just any artist? When was this? How come—"

"Laura!" Holly yelled. "Chill your ass down! How can I think when you're firing a thousand questions at me?"

McCallister remained impatiently silent while Holly scoured her mind. Eventually, she remembered that the man definitely requested her and that he was very specific about what he wanted. She never spoke with him, only to the gallery owner, Gale. She at one point had been confused about the white plant stick with some code on it that he wanted next to the pot. She asked Gale to have him call her, but instead he simply faxed the gallery with the code written large enough to fill the page. She concluded, "Then when I finished, I took the painting to the gallery. He picked it up, said it was beautiful, and paid double the price. I'm sure I told you about that. It was so cool."

"When, Hol? Do you remember when?"

"I think it was summer," she recalled. "So probably almost a year ago. I'll call Gale in the morning and have her look it up. Satisfied?"

"For the moment," McCallister said. "But please call her as soon as you can. Otherwise, I'm going over there. This could be important … or something as simple as the guy passing the painting on to Mr. Faraday because he loved orchids so much. We'll find out."

"Now, shut up and eat," Holly ordered with a chopstick full of Moo Shu Pork.

Eventually, white take-out cartons littered the area and each wine glass had been emptied. In a twist that made two bodies look like one, they fell asleep.

At eleven, McCallister was roused by the sound of her cell phone ringing. The sound was distant, dreamlike, and so she simply nestled back into Holly. Minutes later, the ringing came again, this time forcing her to fly out of bed and down the hall. She rummaged through the pile of her abandoned clothes at the front door. "McCallister!" she finally shouted into the phone.

"It's Peter," he said. "For the fourth time, it's Peter."

She apologized for not hearing his call the first time.

"I've got the autopsy completed," he announced.

McCallister's grogginess swiftly abated with the onslaught of adrenaline. "Tell me!"

"Well, it was definitely poison, a mix of Malathion and Dichlorvos, two pesticides he had on hand," he explained. "It would have taken quite a bit, but his age would have been a factor, too. The process would have been agonizing, and respiratory arrest is what finally killed him."

McCallister thought for a moment and then asked, "How much is quite a bit, Peter? Would he have just drunk it like that without knowing something was wrong?"

"Good question, Laura," Hastings remarked, sounding almost proud of her analytical mind. "I talked with his family physician this evening. He said Faraday had anosmia, which is the inability to smell. Oftentimes, it impairs flavor discrimination. Soda pop or poison—he probably couldn't tell the difference."

"So the sister did do it to him. The bitch!" she spat.

"I have something else for you to add, too. You'll like this one," he said. "We found bloody skin under his fingernails. The DNA matches the DNA we got from the lipstick print on a napkin in the dining room. I'll want a sample from the sister directly, but there's no doubt Faraday was very closely related to whomever he scratched."

McCallister roared, "Damn, you're good, Hastings!"

"No, *you're* good," he countered. "Maine. Maine. Maine. I know how you loathe letting Holly down, so I called in every single favor I have ever been owed to get this testing to the top of the list! Just to get you on that plane. You owe me so big, you'll never be able to make good."

She laughed heartily. "Yeah, but it took you thirty-four years to finally get me in this position! Don't be too proud of yourself. The tables will turn again. They always do."

"You are impossible, Laura!" he wailed. "Now, go back to bed and meet me in my office at seven. I'll give you what you need."

"You get some sleep, too," she scolded. "And, Peter … thank you! I do owe you big." She hung up, denying him the chance to say anything else.

She sat there motionless for several minutes. Her mind methodically listed everything she could possibly turn over to the district attorney. Indeed, it seemed like more than enough. Emphatically, she slapped her stomach several times. "Stop gnawing now! Knot, go away. It's over," she ordered.

Quickly, she punched numbers into her cell phone. "Sorry to wake you, Claudia, but I need to speak with your little woman," she said.

After a half-hearted reprimand for calling so late, Kate's voice came through the phone, "This better be good, Laura."

"This isn't Laura," McCallister clarified. "This is an unnamed source, and this unnamed source is telling you that Faraday was poisoned, murdered. No arrests yet. If you hang out at the coroner's office in the morning around seven, the unnamed source may get a name, and you may get a jump on the others." She paused to make sure the information sank into Kate's groggy mind. After a respectable passage of time, she yelled, "Now quit bothering me and let me get some sleep." Smiling, she ended the call.

She scooped up her pile of clothes and headed back to the bedroom. When she snuggled into Holly, she whispered, "Maine, honey. I think I can get us to Maine."

# Chapter 6

With the sun barely on the rise, McCallister quickly stabbed the button to stop her cell phone alarm from waking Holly. She stroked her hair as she thought about the day ahead. Then she wondered where would the next sunrise find them. A hotel in a different state? Or here, in a funky state of mind? She kissed her softly on the neck and promptly headed to the shower.

The aroma of fresh coffee accosted her when she left the bathroom. She followed it to find Holly busy in the kitchen. Stealthily, she attempted to approach her silk-robed body from behind.

"Slick," Holly barked when McCallister came within four feet of her. "So very slick you are. You were going to slip away without letting me do my community service work." She spun around and wielded a butter knife at her. "I get karma points for taking care of the local detective. Now, sit down!" With the knife, she pointed to an island stool.

McCallister defied her and moved closer, only to receive a swat. "Don't mess with me, Laura," she snarled. "Sit down!" Then, she attempted the most evil look she could, but it failed quickly, becoming a springboard for laughter.

Thinking she had been given a reprieve, McCallister again inched toward her. This time, an outstretched hand stopped her. "You will not come within three feet of me! You know what will happen, what always happens. I mean really! Have you ever had breakfast in the last ten years?" She paused to let them both laugh. "Today is big, so we're going to pretend we're normal. 'Here's your breakfast, honey.' 'Why thank you, dear.' 'Have a good day at work, darling.' 'You have a good day, too, love muffin.'"

"Yes, love muffin, have a good day at home trying to keep your panties on!" McCallister roared.

Composure was completely lacking when the toaster popped its bagel. Holly promptly buttered it and handed a plate and a cup of coffee to McCallister. "Here's your breakfast, honey. Now, shut up and eat it."

"Why thank you, dear."

After the laughter dissipated, McCallister gave her the gist of her conversation with Hastings as she slugged the coffee and picked at the bagel. She tried not to get Holly's hopes up about their vacation, and yet, she felt her own rising. She dressed and headed to the front door. Despite the line she was expected to deliver from the 'normal' script, she simply turned to look at her, intently holding her gaze. The moment suddenly turned serious.

"I love you, Hol," she said.

"I love you, too, babe."

———◆———

McCallister pulled into the parking lot of the coroner's office with fifteen minutes to spare. She caught up with Kate at the front of the building, and they shared a cigarette as the clock wended its way to seven. Both were respectful of the situation, crossing no lines and pressing for no information. As McCallister opened the door to the building, Kate said, "Just to warn you: my colleagues are all camped out at the station. … And thanks."

"Don't mention it, and I do mean don't mention it." She smiled and headed off to see Hastings.

With a jolt, she caught a glimpse of him. "Let me see your feet," she demanded.

He stomped his feet, pointed, looked at them, and then stared at her with confusion. "What? Aren't my shoes polished good enough for you?"

"Actually," she said, "I was looking for toe tags. You look like hell, Hastings."

He shook his head at her and led the way to his desk. There, they went over everything he said to her on the phone the night before. He noted that the green bottle from the greenhouse bench contained both Malathion and Dichlorvos. The identical mix was found in the snifter and Faraday's system. "As you no doubt recall, his stomach contents were on the floor, but I found enough food in his small intestine to determine that his digestion slowed considerably about two to three hours after eating. The chemicals and the alcohol would have slowed the process, as well, but that with temp, rigor, and livor indicate that time of death was between ten and midnight. Probably closer to ten."

"So you're saying he probably suffered for three hours or more?"

Her eyes widened.

"Yes, he could have. He also could have been unconscious and convulsive for most of it. His blood alcohol was .07, so he was extremely close to being legally intoxicated. Maybe that was a blessing."

"Okay, then, give me another one of your educated guesses," McCallister challenged. "Would he have been in any condition to be loudly arguing with his sister at eight-thirty?"

"Well, you're right, it's a guess," he affirmed. "The effects of the poison would not have been immediate. Alcohol would have slowed digestion. He could have been. He would have been drunk ... and more than likely higher than .07."

She nodded with understanding and then asked about the skin under his fingernails.

Hastings explained, "The amount was quite substantial, so whoever he scratched most definitely has obvious wounds. I'll need a warrant for the sister's DNA as well as an exam to find those wounds before they have any further chance to heal. It's already been about thirty-six hours."

Again, McCallister nodded. She also acknowledged the need to move swiftly. "Give me what you've got. I'm going to run everything I've got by the DA ... just as a courtesy."

"Relax, Laura," Hastings said. "You're worried this all looks like a rush job so you can catch that plane, aren't you?" He waited for some admission, but she offered none. "You don't do shoddy work, Laura, and neither do I. But go ahead; run it by Sharon. You know her. She'll laugh you out of her office if you can't give her enough for a solid case, much less an arrest warrant."

She knew that to be truth. Anyone in the department didn't so much as look Sharon Pierce without perfect dots above all i's and flawlessly horizontal crosses on all t's. And even then, they held their breath.

"Go!" he directed with a point of his finger. "I need that DNA and pictures of those scratches—and I needed them last week."

McCallister left the building and officially confirmed to Kate what she had told her the night before. With a devious smile, she watched her hit the button on her PDA to send the pre-written story to her paper. "Nothing more from me for a while," she told her. As she moved toward the street, she yelled back to her. "Do you know Officer Jansen?" When Kate nodded, she offered, "He's got a busy morning ahead of him. I wonder where he's going."

With that clue planted, she crossed the street and hightailed it to Sharon Pierce's office.

"You've got her," Sharon said after McCallister gave her a rundown of the evidence they had gathered. "I'll have no problem getting an arrest warrant, and a jury will have no sympathy for someone who killed her own brother." She paused, staring at McCallister and thinking. "I believe you're right, though, to slow it down so she doesn't lawyer up right away. See what you can get out of her first. You've got probable cause to get a warrant for the DNA and a cursory exam—both are must-haves for me. I'll even call ahead for you." She scanned her desk calendar. "It's Judge Miller. He'll have it signed before you even make it to his clerk's office. When you need an arrest warrant, just call me." Confidently, she nodded. "Good work, Detective."

Half an hour later, McCallister passed through the throng outside the station with each reporter firing a question at her. This time the local press had expanded to include two national crews and several from outlying areas. Faraday Paper attracted attention, as did its heirs. She confirmed the cause of death and stressed that no arrests had been made.

Then, she eagerly sought out Jansen and Jessop to share the autopsy results with them.

"You still want to haul her ass in, Jansen?"

He grinned and nodded emphatically.

"Do it," she said. "For questioning."

With an evil twinkle in his eye, he rubbed his hands together and spun on his heels. For all the evidence they had, McCallister felt most bolstered by Jansen's utter disdain for Alexandra Sinclair. His instincts about people were usually dead on; when someone raised the hair on his neck, she paid attention.

In hot pursuit of coffee, McCallister entered the break room to find Captain Greeley in mid-pour. He smiled and offered the cup to her when he finished filling it. As he poured another, he asked, "Are you going to make that plane, Laura?"

"I wish I could tell you, Cap," she replied. "One minute it seems like I will, and then, it seems virtually impossible."

"You don't have to stay, you know. We're quite capable," he assured with a laugh. "Except it would probably kill you to walk away." He took a drink of his coffee and then leaned in as though he was about to confide in her. "It's kind of sick about us cops that way. We work our tails off to keep the city safe, and yet, there's that incredible high that comes from stringing the yellow tape and trying to get a dead man to tell us what happened."

She knew what he meant; it was a paradox that baffled her on many occasions. *Don't kill, man, but if you do, I'm there, running as fast as I can.* The whole notion itself seemed like it should be punishable by law, and yet, it was okay—as long motivation began and ended with compassion and requital for the victim. It had to boil down to that. It had to come down to the clouds in Tobias Faraday's eyes. Otherwise, it was demented.

"So before you fill me in on what you've got so far," he hinted with a loud clearing of his throat, "I just want you to know that if your vacation gets jacked up, we'll figure something out. We'll make it work—however we have to. Now, get me up to speed."

Midway through her discourse with Greeley, two shift-change reports were handed to her. One indicated that the only activity at the Faraday house overnight was a light in the guesthouse from eight-thirty to eleven-thirty. The officer noted that his attempts to get an answer at the door proved unsuccessful. The other report pertained to the activity at Alexandra Sinclair's apartment. Here, the officer indicated that a man arrived at 9:00 PM and left at 5:37 AM. Running the license plates produced the name Dominic Vitale. He further stated that her lights came on at 9:04 PM, went off at 10:53 PM, and came on again at 5:02 AM.

McCallister concluded her conversation with Greeley and returned to her desk to work on reports. Soon, she heard a disturbance down the hall.

"Don't rush me, or I'll have your badge, you Neanderthal!" Alexandra Sinclair had obviously entered the building.

McCallister made a quick call to Ristow and headed to the interrogation suite. The observation mirror provided a glimpse of an outraged woman bitching nonstop at Jansen as he rearranged chairs around the table. He pointed at one, and Alexandra sat down forcefully. After Jansen made his exit, she watched her squirm for several minutes and then made her way into the room.

As she set a file and a cup of coffee on the table, Alexandra glared at her. "That officer was rude," she spouted, "Why I couldn't finish putting on my makeup is beyond me. The jackass!"

McCallister smiled graciously at her. "Mrs. Sinclair, I don't think men have any idea what us women must go through to look our best." Before Alexandra had a chance to commiserate, she continued, "The coroner's office has concluded that your brother was poisoned to death, so it's very important that we get our facts straight." She watched Alexandra's jaws tighten, and then she hit the button on the video recorder. "I'm going to record our conversation, Mrs. Sinclair, so that no one can accuse you of saying anything you didn't say." She turned around quickly and looked at Alexandra. "It's for your protection. Just like the Miranda Warning is—" She paused. "Officer Neanderthal read you your rights, didn't he?"

Alexandra shook her head, and McCallister pushed, "The whole 'you have the right to remain silent' spiel—he didn't recite it to you?" When she shook her head again, McCallister flew to the door, flung it open, and bellowed, "Jansen, get in here!"

Swiftly, he moved into the room, looking uncomfortable and confused. McCallister wailed, "I don't care that the law says Miranda Warning is only necessary upon arrest. I've seen too many innocent people railroaded by this system." She paused, seeming to try to regain control of her breathing that was swift and audible. "How the hell many times have I told you that I want anyone I question to be read their rights?" He shrugged, and she commanded, "Do it now, Jansen!"

He promptly did as she instructed, ending with, "Do you understand your rights, Mrs. Sinclair?"

"Of course, I understand," she spat at him. "I'm not the Neanderthal."

McCallister motioned to the door for Jansen to leave, which he eagerly did. "Men, huh?" she remarked to Alexandra and then took a chair across from her. She probed until she got her to say that she was comfortable waiving her rights, that they could talk freely. "Yes, I'm sure you would want to do all you can to find out who killed your brother." She watched Alexandra merely bow her head.

After an uncomfortable moment, McCallister asked, "Why is it, Mrs. Sinclair, that you've never seemed very upset by the idea that someone murdered your brother?"

"Because he was a cantankerous old man," she answered very matter-of-factly. Then, she laughed. "Even when he was a boy, he was a cantankerous old man."

"But you loved him?"

"Of course, I did."

"And your fighting never went beyond sibling spats?"

"No. He was never good at arguing either. Our spats never lasted very long."

"Did he ever hurt you ... become violent?"

"For God's sake, no. I actually think he was afraid of me."

McCallister requested an explanation, and Alexandra expounded, "I think he was jealous of me. I had a life outside that hell hole of a house, and he had nothing."

"It seemed like he had all the money, though. No?" McCallister queried.

"That he did," she replied. "And he was a miser with it, to the point where he lived like a king and I had to live in a slummy apartment."

"Slummy" did not exactly describe her living conditions, but McCallister had something else in mind. "Yes, I talked to Arlen Dorsey, and it sounds like your brother made sure everything went to the botany department at the university with hardly anything to you. What a shame."

"That's not true!" Alexandra shouted. "I just talked to Arlen a few days ago. Everything goes to me!" Her eyes were wild with defiance.

"Oh," McCallister said, stretching the word. "Did he change the will or something? That's not what I heard. Maybe I misunderstood."

"Yes, as a matter of fact, he did change it recently."

"At your request?"

"Actually, I suppose it was. One of the few times he listened to me. He was getting on in years; he was my older brother, you know. He needed to see that those stupid orchids of his meant nothing, that throwing his money to the lazy leeches at the college was utter stupidity. The money should stay in the family. So, yes, he changed his will."

"How convenient," McCallister said as she jotted a couple of notes in her file.

"What the hell is that supposed to mean?" Alexandra yelled. "He was a son-of-a-bitch. Whatever he got he had coming to him. That money is rightfully mine. And frankly, I can't wait to burn every one of his goddamn orchids. Stupid son-of-bitch! Stupid little man. Stupid men!"

With perfectly ill timing, McCallister's cell phone went off in her pocket. She grabbed it and spied Holly's cell number on the screen and chose to ignore it.

"Mrs. Sinclair, remember the conversation we had yesterday about how your fingerprints would be all over your brother's house?"

"Yes," she said, still shaking from her angry outburst.

"Well, your DNA is probably all over as well since you had dinner and drinks with him," she explained. "I'm going to need to get a sample from you so that we can, again, tell what belongs to you and what belongs to someone else."

Alexandra merely scowled at her.

"I'm afraid—" Her cell phone went off again, this time with the text message tone. She glanced, noting that it was from Holly. It simply read, "Painting = Thaddeus Frederick."

McCallister apologized for the interruption. She tried again, "I'm afraid we're going to need a DNA sample from you, like I said, to make sure what belongs to you and what doesn't." She rose and moved to the door.

"This is ridiculous, Detective." She paused. "Perhaps I should call my lawyer."

"That is certainly your right, Mrs. Sinclair. Please do whatever makes you feel comfortable." McCallister pleasantly smiled at her.

"This whole thing makes me uncomfortable. If I did what makes me comfortable, I'd leave."

"Do you want your lawyer? Do you *need* someone's help?" McCallister asked. When she finally shook her head, McCallister asked, "Can I get a DNA sample from you then?"

Alexandra questioned how the sample was taken. Once McCallister reassured her that it was a painless swab inside the mouth and a plucking of hair from her head, she consented. McCallister smiled slightly, knowing that avoiding the use of a warrant assured that she still had the upper hand.

McCallister summoned Ristow and stood quietly while the sample was taken and recorded. As Ristow finished up, McCallister asked, "Mrs. Sinclair, do you have any scratches on your body?"

Alexandra emphatically shook her head, and McCallister said, "I have reason to believe that your brother scratched you the other night, so hard, in fact, that your skin was found under his fingernails during his autopsy." McCallister watched as she squirmed, her face turning red and her hands wildly smoothing her pant legs. "Mrs. Sinclair, I can easily produce a warrant that would allow us to check. It might be in your best interest just to show us."

"Fine!" she finally shouted, pulling up her sleeve and exposing three long gashes. "You're going to twist it into something it's not. I told you he was a cantankerous old man. He was crazy! It was unprovoked! It's not what you think!"

McCallister asked her to hold out her arm so Ristow could take several photographs. As she angrily did so, McCallister asked, "What is it exactly that you think I think, Alexandra?"

The use of her first name did not go unnoticed by Alexandra. She suddenly looked at McCallister with contempt. "You're a goddamn cop. Just like the others. You can quit pretending now. Goddamn cop. You think I killed my poor dear brother."

"Did you, Alex?"

Instead of arguing, she laughed dramatically. "Well, you obviously think so. Does it even matter what I say?"

"It matters to me, Alex." McCallister said calmly. "Think of me what you will, but I really want the person who did this to him, not just somebody to hang it on." Then she moved within an inch of her face. "Do you realize that he suffered for hours after he drank the poison *this person* put in his cognac? Convulsions. Vomiting. Pain. He suffered, Alex! He suffered more than any of us know. And when death finally came for him, it probably felt like a blessing. I want the bastard who would do such a thing to him!" She glared at her.

"See, there it is!" she screamed as she shot up from her chair. "You care about the son-of-a-bitch! Not me—not whether I'm doing what's comfortable or that I'm not accused of something I didn't do. Goddamn liar cop! You care about him! Never me. Always that son-of-a-bitch! Everybody cared for that son-of-a-bitch. Mother and Father, so fucking in love with their little man, their precious little man. Am I glad he's gone? You bet, but I didn't do it!" she yelled, punctuating the denial with fists on the table.

McCallister eagerly showed her hand. "Your prints are on the bottle of poison, on the snifter, on the cognac that you bought that night. You have scratches on your arm. You admit to arguing with him. Even the neighbors heard you arguing. You got him to change his will so everything went to you. He said he was afraid of you, Alex. He was a stupid little man who was afraid of you. And from listening to all this crap you're spewing, I think he was probably right to be afraid of you." She paused long enough to give her a look of disgust. "Yeah, you loved him all right."

Alexandra's eyes grew wide and dark. She stared at McCallister, but McCallister refused to flinch.

"He was your brother, your own flesh and blood! You make me sick, Mrs. Sinclair." She pointed to the chair, told her to sit down, and then waited for her to comply.

"I want my lawyer."

"You *need* your lawyer."

McCallister and Ristow slowly and quietly left the room.

# Chapter 7

McCallister closed the door to the interrogation room and made a beeline down the hall. Greeley, who had apparently watched the entire interrogation, gave her a confident thumbs-up. "Good job, Laura," he said. "You got everything but a signed confession, and I really thought you were about to get one. Motive up the wazoo. I'll call Sharon."

She waved at him and then darted into the bathroom. Hurrying into the last stall and falling to her knees, she vomited. She knelt there until her stomach stopped roiling and her face stopped sweating. She stood for a moment to brace herself, and upon exiting, she almost ran face-first into Ristow.

"Are you okay, Laura?" she asked with visible concern.

McCallister smiled. "Well, you really mustn't think so if you called me by my first name," she quipped. "Only Greeley does that around here."

Ristow put her hand out and waited for reciprocation. Smiling, the two shook hands.

"Laura, nice to meet you. My name is Leigh," she said. "Now, are you all right?"

She laughed. "Yes, Leigh. I'm just fine. Anger just has that effect on my stomach sometimes."

"I hear you," she reassured.

"I used to think it was weakness. Now I either know better, or I've deluded myself into thinking that it's just getting other people's evil out of my system. Whatever."

"Are you sure you're okay? Can I get you anything?"

"As a matter of fact, there this. Get my evidence to the lab!"

Ristow laughed. "Yes, you are just fine! As bossy as ever." She clutched her collection kit and camera and sped out the door.

McCallister washed up and then strode back into the hallway to find Jansen waiting for her. "Did I do something wrong, Detective? Should I really have read her her rights?"

"Damn, I wish you'd trust me, Jansen," she said. "If I was going to yell at you for a screw-up, I sure as hell wouldn't do it in front of a suspect."

"Oh, I suppose not," he said, his body relaxing and a smile making its way across his face.

"She didn't need to be Mirandized. I just wanted the path of least resistance with her. It was probably wasted energy, but it certainly didn't hurt," she explained. "Can you make sure she gets a call to her lawyer?"

"Already taken care of. He's on his way. She also said she's diabetic and needs lunch, so I took care of that, too," he boasted. "And Greeley says he wants to see you."

She thanked him and headed to the captain's office. She found him seated at his desk, just hanging up the phone. "Everything is set," he said. "Her lawyer's on the way. Sharon said to go for it. So I want you to grab lunch, get as much of your paperwork done as possible, and get the hell out of here."

"Are you sure?" she asked. Even after he nodded vigorously, she added, "Positive?"

"What is the big deal, Laura?" he asked, obviously confused by her unusual behavior. "You've got her. Case closed. Get out of here."

McCallister left his office, and then with her jacket in hand, she snuck out the back of the building to avoid the press. She took a spot on the grass that spring was coaxing the green back into. She lit a cigarette, inhaled, and then exhaled so deeply that it made her lightheaded. Willfully, she tried to clear her mind, but it wouldn't stop its churning. She thought of Holly, and a sudden need to wrap her arms around her, to feel her love, consumed her.

Quickly, she grabbed her cell, thumbed "I love you," sent it, and then waited. The cell's irritating tone would tell her that Holly was there and that she felt the same way. Minutes passed, and still the text message remained unanswered. She fidgeted. She worried. She checked the cell's signal bars and power. And finally the tone told her what she needed to know. "I love you, too," the message read.

Then seconds later, the cell sounded again. "Eat lunch!"

"Pack!" she thumbed back to her.

"Serious?"

"Yes!"

The to-and-fro text messages ended with both a smiley face and another "I love you!" from Holly.

Recharged, she headed back to her desk to get as much paperwork done as she could. The area was bustling with activity—activity she knew would have been her doing and responsibility had there not been the state of Maine. She glanced up as a confident Jansen escorted Alexandra Sinclair out of interrogation in the direction of booking with Arlen Dorsey in hot pursuit. She saw Jessop in the group, giving her a salute and a smile in passing. She endured the nasty glare from Faraday's sister, and in her mind, she tried to imagine the clouds evaporating from his eyes. It was a horrid end, but at least in that end, there were words given to describe his demise.

And through it all, there was a gnawing knot in the pit of her stomach.

Greeley approached to ask whether or not she wanted to take care of the press conference or if she wanted him to do it. Normally, that official announcement provided closure for her, but this time she hesitated. First, she thought to tell him to do it; he loved the media spotlight when there were positive things to say about his department. Then, she conceded, "I'll take care of it."

The media nearly mobbed her as she approached the curb.

"Alexandra Sinclair has just been arrested for the murder of her brother, Tobias Faraday," she announced.

She watched as Kate instantaneously hit a button on her PDA, again a pre-written piece made its way to the *Granton Journal* after confirmation was had. Knowing Kate as she did, she was sure the article was riddled with facts about Alexander Sinclair, things she had researched after she had probably followed Jansen to the apartment complex that morning. She didn't smile, but she wanted to.

She answered all the press' questions that she could and then headed back to the paperwork. At four-thirty, she handed Greeley what she had, grabbed her jacket, and made for home.

Holly enthusiastically greeted her at the door, her level of excitement bordering on frenzy. McCallister knew that it stemmed from more than the simple prospect of Maine. It was the last-second seizure of something almost dropped. It was the final downhill slope of a nauseating roller coaster ride. It was victory, and that became sorely evident when Holly offered high-fives.

"You're good, Detective!" she declared. "I'm very proud of you. I really didn't think you could do it, and not because I doubted you. Just because time was definitely not on your side."

McCallister gently tugged her into the living room and brought them both to a horizontal position on the couch. She wrapped her arms around her and just drifted into the solace. It was good there. It was safe.

"So who killed the poor old guy, babe?" Holly asked after several minutes of silence.

"His sister."

"And that makes you sad," she put forward without question.

"Yes," she readily confirmed. "Doesn't it make you sad?"

"Yes, it makes me sad, too. I think I would have liked him. I don't know why I think that. Maybe just the painting." She paused. "Who is Thaddeus Frederick anyway?"

"He's the guy who lives in Faraday's guesthouse."

"Would I like him, too?" she asked. "I mean aside from the fact that he liked my work so much that he doubled my commission."

"I don't know, Hol," McCallister flatly responded. "I've never met him. No one has, actually."

"Well, I bet I'd like him," she deduced and then asked, "Are you hungry, babe? I'd bet my life that you never had lunch."

McCallister informed her that she wanted nothing more than a hot shower and a glass of wine. Reluctantly, they got up from the couch.

Holly brought her wine while McCallister readied to shower. Holly hoped that the combination of those two things would bring her lover fully back to her. McCallister hovered in a different place—a place Holly recognized from afar as one common to her murder investigations. She knew from experience that her job now was to wait it out, to gently coax her back, and to be there for her when she arrived.

Indeed, she seemed more like herself after the shower. She continued to sip her wine as they rechecked their luggage and prepared the house for their absence. McCallister checked the outside of the house and made sure the cars were locked. Holly checked appliances and shoved snacks into her carry-on. They sat by the front door, going through tickets and itineraries, when a car horn blared. A moment later, Kate and Claudia stood at the door with outstretched hands looking for luggage to carry.

"Thanks, you two, for offering to get us to the airport," Holly said, giving them both a hug and a kiss.

McCallister and Kate loaded the trunk, while Holly and Claudia gabbed like only best friends could do. Eventually, the foursome was maneuvering through Friday night traffic with Kate at the wheel. She pulled to the curb at the airport, and the whole packing and gabbing routine ran its reverse course. Holly and Claudia had a drawn-out goodbye, as if years instead of days were about to pass.

Half an hour later, McCallister and Holly sat in the boarding area with nearly an hour to kill. They sat in silence for several minutes until Holly retrieved a small bag of potato chips from her carry-on. "If you eat this entire bag for me, I'll kiss you right here and now, in front of all these people," she challenged.

"Hol, that sounds more like a threat than an incentive," McCallister countered. "Besides, I don't want any of these people watching you kiss me."

"All right, then, party pooper. What'll it take?"

"How about a simple 'please'?"

"Babe, would you please eat these potato chips? It would make me very happy."

She smiled at her and took the bag, deciding to ignore the gnawing knot in her stomach and just eat the blasted things. Holly grabbed some glam magazine from her bag, and McCallister went for the *American Orchidist Association Magazine* she had stashed in her own. She leafed through the pages, viewing picture after picture of incredible flowers. Holly slowly became interested and leaned in. McCallister could sense her artist's mind appraising the different hues and angles of light.

Suddenly, Holly stabbed a page. "That's the kind of flower I painted for that guy," she declared. She read the caption and then affirmed, "A cattleya! Isn't it beautiful?"

It was indeed beautiful and very, very close to how Holly had rendered it on canvas. Her talents amazed Laura. They had started dating when she was a mere eighteen years old, when she was still searching inside for unfettered access to her fount of creativity. Now, at twenty-nine, she owned it, drank it, submerged herself in it. She was truly gifted.

When Holly's eyes returned to an article on depilatories or some such craved wisdom in her own magazine, McCallister scanned the index of the orchid magazine. When she saw the word "cataloguing," she flipped to the specified page. "Cataloguing a Collection," the title read. To her, it was like reading a foreign language, and the idea of cataloguing seemed like trying to find a book in the library with a reverse Dewey decimal system: knowing the code would lead to the book title.

Instead of trying to understand what was truly beyond her, she skimmed the article for mention of Mr. Faraday. "Tobias Faraday, lifelong resident of Granton, has been deeply involved with orchids since his adolescence," a portion stated. She read a description of his command center and the layout of his greenhouse. She read the descriptions of many of the flowers she had walked past in her quest for understanding of what had happened to him.

Then, she encountered a paragraph that forced the gnawing in her stomach to reach a fever pitch. "As a neighbor and confidante of Faraday, I have enjoyed learning the ins and outs of cataloguing a collection the way he does. He told me, 'Even with hundreds of plants, you get to know them individually, and I've even taken them into consideration when preparing my will. The catalogue becomes like a very personal history. There is no system that can take the place of careful, handwritten accounts of life and death.'"

The gnawing knot writhed with a life its own, intermittently seizing her insides like a tourniquet. "Something's not right," she mumbled as her hands flicked the article's pages back to the first. "Something's not right!"

"What, babe?"

"Something's not right, Holly. I missed something. I screwed up!" Frantically, she looked at the title page again. "'Cataloguing a Collection by T. A. Frederick.'"

"Laura, what's wrong?"

She fumbled in her pocket for her cell and tried to settle her mind enough to remember a phone number. "I missed something, Hol! I know this sounds insane, but Faraday's still trying to tell me something. I can't goddamn hear him, Hol!" She stabbed the numbers, and in mid-greeting, she yelled, "Jansen, what exactly was the name on the mailbox at Faraday's guesthouse? ... Thank you." She hung up before he had a chance to ask what she was up to or when her plane took off. *The plane!* she thought.

"Laura, talk to me. You're acting goofy. Tell me what the hell is going on!"

"Thaddeus Frederick, the guy in the guesthouse. Thaddeus A. Frederick. T. A. Frederick!" she spouted. "Faraday's neighbor, his confidante. Read this, Holly!" She pointed to the paragraph and waited until she finished. "Does that sound like a man who would suddenly leave all his orchids to his cold-hearted sister? Why not just the money? Why the orchids, too? She told me today that she couldn't wait to burn the things."

"The bitch!" Holly spat. "But if she's in jail, she can't. Can she?"

"Well, she could if she got bail or was found not guilty, but right now, that's not the point," she said, her mind still racing. "He loved those things. He wouldn't do it. And if nothing 'can take the place of careful, handwritten accounts or life or death,' where the hell are all his journals, Hol? We found one, only half-used. He didn't just start. He's nearly OCD when it comes to writing everything down! Where the hell are his journals, honey?" She abruptly stood and flattened her hands over her mouth. "I missed something, Hol. What if the sister didn't do it? What if I did railroad an innocent person?"

"Laura, chill your ass down," Holly yelled. "You act like you put her in the gas chamber today. She's a bitch. She's sitting in jail. Isn't that what those— What are they called? Probable hearings? Preliminaries?" When McCallister nodded, she continued, "Doesn't she have to have one of those? Didn't you say that it basically checks your work, that it makes sure you have enough on somebody? If you're wrong, she's free, isn't she? Big damn deal. Let her sit."

"There is enough evidence, though, Holly. Chances are very good the preliminary hearing will result in her being bound over for trial. The DA thinks she's even got enough to convict her."

"But still, you're acting like that already happened, babe. It hasn't."

Suddenly, their boarding call came over the PA. McCallister fidgeted and grabbed her bag. Holly fumbled for her own, keeping her eyes glued to McCallister the entire time. "Let's just not go, Laura. Then you can figure out whatever you think is wrong." She paused briefly and then braved, "Do you really think he's talking to you?"

She chuckled, and Holly felt reassured.

"No, he doesn't talk to me, but he was alive just the other day. He wrote notes. He made dinner and set a table. He kept a journal. He hung paintings. There are a million ways that the dead tell their story, describe who they are. I think I missed something really big."

"Then like I said, let's just skip Maine. Let's stay here."

"No!" Laura yelled and began pulling her toward the gate. "This is important to you, to us. Let's go. I'll call Greeley during our layover in Boston. I'll see what he can do."

They got their tickets scanned and then entered the tunnel to the plane. The line moved swiftly. At least it did until Holly grabbed McCallister's jacket and refused to move one step further. McCallister tugged, but Holly still refused, digging in her heels as people from behind pushed and elbowed.

"I'm not going, Laura. You can go if you've got something to prove, but I'm not going."

"Holly, don't do this. We're going to Maine!" she yelled back at her, while trying to pull her out of the flow of traffic. "Come on!"

"Do you want me to cause a scene?" she dared, and McCallister knew that was well within her abilities. "You don't get it, do you? Big shot detective and you can't even see what's in front of your face." She spread out her fingers and flashed her hand in McCallister's face. "You seem to think the world revolves around me. Well, I've got news for you, love muffin! It does, indeed. But you're standing there right next to me. And when you're not happy, I'm not happy. When your world's not right, mine's not right either." Her eyes suddenly welled with tears. "I don't care about Maine. Actually, I'm getting to the point where I hate Maine. I'm sick of it. I'd sit in a dumpster for a week as long as you were with me. If we go to Maine, you won't be with me, babe. Your head will be here. I'd rather stay here and be with you than go there with you and still not have you. If that makes any sense."

McCallister pulled her into an embrace, only to realize that the tunnel was now deserted, except for an airline worker on each end, staring suspiciously at them. "Sorry to slow things up," she said. Then, she moved back from Holly, looked her squarely in the eyes, and said, "Last chance, Hol. What do you want? I'll give you whatever you want."

Tears streamed down her face. "I want to be with you. That's all this vacation was ever about. You and me. I want to be with you wherever that is. And if that's here, I swear, babe, it's okay. Do what you've got to do. I just want to be with you."

McCallister was torn and dealing with her own tears. It didn't matter to her where they were, either, as long as they were together. "Okay," she said. "You're right. My head will be here, and that's not fair to you. My heart is always with you, though. I love you." Again, she became aware of suspicious eyes staring at them. She grabbed Holly's hand and started heading back into the terminal. "We've changed our minds," she said to the worker who had scanned them in. "We're staying home. Sorry for the trouble."

They made a beeline for the counter and asked the worker if they could get their luggage off the plane that was about to depart. He looked at his computer terminal and said, "I'm sorry. It's already on board, and the plane is about to leave." He asked for their tickets, punched some keys on his keyboard, and informed them, "I can have your luggage held in Boston and flown back on the next available flight." He paused. "It looks like it would be back here tomorrow afternoon." He handed them a form, which McCallister began to fill out immediately.

Holly elbowed her and said, "At least now I have a socially acceptable reason for not wearing panties. They're all in Boston for a tea party."

They both laughed, and while the airlines worker's crimson face should have restrained them, it only made them laugh harder. Holly giddily excused herself, leaving McCallister to contend with the man's utter embarrassment. As she walked away, she said, "I'll see if I can get Kate and Claudia to come back and get our sorry asses."

Soon, they were outside in the chilly April night. They sat on a bench and waited for their friends. McCallister smoked a cigarette and churned things in her mind. She decided that above all else, she needed to speak with the elusive T. A. Frederick.

When Kate and Claudia arrived to pick them up, they dealt with an onslaught of questions. Holly grabbed Claudia and began gabbing again, while Kate approached McCallister and lit her own cigarette to join her.

"What's the deal, Laura?" Kate asked. "If it has anything to do with the case, I swear I can listen and keep my mouth shut. You know you can trust me."

"I do know that," McCallister affirmed. "So off the record ... I think I missed something, and I need to keep looking. When you were at the scene yesterday, I assume you did your job and interviewed people in the neighborhood." Kate nodded, and McCallister asked, "Did you learn anything about the guy who lives in the Faraday guesthouse?"

Kate smiled broadly. "You know, when you told me that Officer Jansen was going somewhere this morning, I would have bet my life that's where he was going to lead me. I really thought it had to be Frederick because it was like he didn't even exist. Nobody knew a damn thing about him, and it bothered everybody. People a block away knew the story. What a smart way to get away with murder. Nobody's ever seen you; yet, there you are right in the crime scene's backyard."

McCallister nodded in acknowledgement of Kate's reasoning. "I need to find this guy even if I have to sit on the doorstep for the next six months." She retrieved the magazine from her bag and tossed it to her. "Page thirty-seven, marked with a piece of paper," she instructed. "Read the author's name and then read the last page of the article."

She gave her time to complete the task, and then she asked her the same questions she had asked Holly, questions she still asked herself. Why did he change the will so that the orchids went to his sister and not just the money? Where were his journals? And who the hell was the invisible man in the guesthouse who penned the article?

# Chapter 8

To Holly's utter amazement and delight, McCallister got into the car and announced that she was famished. The four of them shared a meal and liberating laughter at a diner not far from the airport. It recharged them and turned the idea of missing out on vacation into utter nonsense. Holly could sense that McCallister was close again, and she vowed to tether her a little tighter this time.

Once back in the city, Kate asked McCallister if she wanted her to drive past the Faraday place to see if Frederick was at home. McCallister reasoned that a mere check on the guesthouse would do no harm. Getting the go-head, Kate made her way to the Faraday house, which proved to be foreboding in the dark of night. She pulled the car so they could spy a look to the far back. There was the guesthouse ... lights blazing.

Like a shark sensing blood in the water, she ordered Kate to pull into the back alley as she wildly rummaged through her bag to retrieve her badge. She informed them that if she got an answer at the door that she would immediately call for backup. Holly asked her whether she had her gun, and when she said that she didn't, Holly shrieked, "What if he's the murderer? Are you stupid?"

"I don't think he is, Hol."

Claudia challenged what she thought to be poor judgment. "And what caliber is your assumption, Detective?"

"I just need to do this," she quickly concluded as she exited the car. Then, she directed Kate to pull a safe distance down the alley.

With a badge in one hand and her cell phone in the other, McCallister approached the front door and knocked loudly. "Mr. Frederick, I'm Detective McCallister of the Granton Police Department," she yelled. "I need to speak with you, sir." When no answer came, she repeated the routine three more times to no avail.

She ran back to the car and asked if they had a flashlight. Claudia popped the trunk; McCallister swiftly grabbed the flashlight and headed back. Carefully, she walked the parameter of the small house, trying to get a look in a window. As she did so, she yelled Frederick's name repeatedly. When she got to the backside of the house, she noticed a drape that was not drawn completely, leaving enough of a gap to provide a glimpse inside. She neared the window, still yelling his name, and then she froze in her tracks. She dialed dispatch.

"This is Detective Laura McCallister," she said and then quickly provided her badge number and her location. She spouted the police codes to indicate a possible dead body and her need for assistance. "I am outside the residence. I do not have my weapon." She listened until she could hear the dispatcher in the background passing her message to a cop via radio. Then she made a mad dash to the car, covering the phone, and yelling to Kate, "There's a body. Backup's coming. Get the hell out of here, *now!*" She banged her fist on the top of the car and shouted, "Go!"

When the car sped safely out of sight, she returned to the guesthouse. She checked the front door and windows to find them all locked. Quickly, she returned to the front door and started trying to bash it in with her shoulders, but it did not give. She knew she was capable of defending herself against a physical attack, but if an armed perp was inside, she realized she was in a jam. Then, she heard her name being called on her cell and brought it to her ear. A patrol car was within two minutes.

She headed to the alley and waited, minding the house while searching for approaching lights. Soon, a squad approached, and McCallister held out her badge for the officers to see the headlight beams. Promptly, they exited the vehicle, and she filled them in on the situation. With a small battering ram proving itself more formidable than McCallister's shoulder, the front door was quickly wide open. The officers entered the house with guns drawn, while McCallister waited, feeling like an idiot for having jumped into the situation is such an unprepared way. When the all-clear came, she made her way in and headed to the back.

"I think you'll want to see this, Detective."

She entered the small bedroom, turned to peer into its bathroom, and realized the body she had seen from the window was simply a dressed-up mannequin. It was fully clothed and sported a blond and gray peppered wig and matching mustache. There was even a dried pool adjacent to it that resembled blood.

"Would one of you please radio and get me a CSU team?" McCallister asked. "And do *not* make any jokes that a lifeless mannequin does not a crime scene make. Somebody is messing with us, and I want to know who."

She stared at the mannequin and then moved back to the window, studying angles, making sure she hadn't overreacted. The perspective from the window offered only a view of the lower torso and the dried pool. She reasoned that anyone would have assumed it was an actual body. She returned to the bathroom and stared some more.

After requesting and receiving a pair of gloves from an officer, she pulled them on, straddled the mannequin, and reached into its back pocket— just as she would have done to a human. From the pocket, her hand retrieved a thin, brown wallet. She carefully flipped it open to find a card. It read: *Mr. Probable Cause.*

What coursed through her was an unbalanced mix of anger and intrigue. Someone intentionally afforded her reasonable grounds to enter the premises without a warrant. She had been duped only to receive a coveted prize: She was standing in the residence of T. A. Frederick. Did she have probable cause to search, now that it was determined there was no body, no threat, no crime? Playing it safe, she carefully set down the wallet and scurried in pursuit anything in plain sight.

Her mind expeditiously tried to absorb the entirety of the scene. The rooms were immaculate; not a thing seemed out of place. And then, she realized that things were actually a scarcity. There was nothing on the bedroom dresser … nothing on the bathroom sink or in the medicine cabinet … nothing on the counters in the tiny makeshift kitchen area. Nothing. A shell. An empty house with furniture … and a plastic dead man named Mr. Probable Cause.

Her insides screamed in frustration. Maybe the coveted prize should never have been coveted. But, why had someone gone to this extent simply to allow her entry—someone who knew procedure? What the hell was she supposed to see?

She decided to head outside to wait for CSU. Cool air and a cigarette would help her clear her head, and she could call Holly to tell her there was no danger. As she passed through the living area to the front door, her moment of epiphany arrived in all its splendor. On the small table at the front of the house, innocently sat a leather-bound book with the initials "TAF" boldly embossed in gold on the cover. Instantly, she remembered Faraday's journal she had clutched the day before, the one that detailed the moments before his sister arrived to snuff out his mortal existence, the one now sitting in an evidence bag.

"Tobias A. Faraday," she said aloud. Then with a feeling of triumphant defeat, she added, "Thaddeus A. Frederick."

Hardly befitting the situation at hand, she let out a robust laugh that shook the night while "TAF" seared itself indelibly into her brain. The two officers snapped their heads around to look at her.

"Frederick is Faraday," she said, not caring that it made no sense to them; it made sense to her. "I'd stake my reputation on it."

And she knew that she was about to. If Frederick was Faraday, then they were both dead and muted, and that elusive thing she chased might still prove to be her own tail.

She looked to the leather-bound book again, wanting nothing more than to open it and spy its trove. Smartly, though, she knew that paramount to that was a good set of prints from it, perfect matches to Faraday. She told the officers that they could head to their squad and take off as soon as CSU arrived.

Eagerly, she continued the mission that had been so profoundly interrupted: fresh air, a smoke, and a call to Holly. She claimed a spot on the lawn a safe distance from the house and lit a cigarette. Willfully, she tried to slow her racing mind, and then she stabbed speed dial on her cell, knowing that Holly's ringtone was about to startle the three of them.

Hearing Holly's voice eased her heart and her gyrating mind. She explained that there was no body and no danger and that she needed to wait for CSU to do their work before she could leave. She told Holly to have Kate and Claudia drive her home, that she would get a ride and join her as soon as she could. An argumentative Holly and two just as argumentative voices in the background quickly decided that was not acceptable to them. They would hit a drive-thru for beverages and then wait for her a block down from Faraday's house. McCallister thought it was a ludicrous idea, but the sudden disconnection sound in her ear left her little sway in the debate.

Finally, CSU arrived, and she fired orders at them. She wanted pictures, fingerprints from at least a dozen locations, and a sample of the substance under the mannequin. First on her list, however, was lifting any prints off the book on the table.

Like a child on Christmas morning, she hovered near the night shift's version of Leigh Ristow. The tech's gray powder and lifting tape worked their magic, retrieving an entire flawless handprint from the front cover. The rest of the book was print-free.

When she was given the go-ahead, she excitedly and carefully pulled the book open. "The Journal of Thaddeus A. Frederick," the first page read. With the innumerable samples of Faraday's handwriting, there was no doubt in McCallister's mind that the lab would make a match. She turned the next page to discover not answers to her questions, but merely another clue. It was one of those orchid codes from Faraday's command center. She borrowed paper and a pen from a tech and transcribed, "ChaMys.04.79.425.x58x66."

She stared at the piece of paper from different angles, as if a certain perspective would magically allow the code to transform into something that made sense to her. Again, she knew that the reverse Dewey was smarter than she. As she thought, she looked to her watch. Was eleven-fifteen on a Friday night considered as late as the same time on a weekday? She hoped not as she stabbed speed dial again, this time asking Holly to read her the phone number on the piece of paper in the orchid magazine.

A minute later, Dr. Marty Spangler voiced his greeting.

"This is Detective Laura McCallister. I'm sorry for calling so late, but you offered your help, and I am in desperate need of it," she explained.

A plan developed to have Dr. Spangler and three trusted students meet her at Faraday's house the next morning at nine. By utilizing his expertise, she intended to have him decipher the code she held in her hand and every single one that hung in Faraday's command center. If this all came down to an orchid, she needed his direction in order to traverse a coded greenhouse.

After ending the call, she jotted a few notes, and then suddenly the guesthouse went pitch-black. Everyone froze in place. Protection of the scene was so instinctual that no one had bothered to turn on any additional lights. She hit the button on her flashlight, shone it on the wall, and hit the light switch. Nothing. She flipped it several more times and then started going from light to light, finding them all out of commission—except for the one that had allowed her visage of the mannequin. She quickly discovered that the light was on an automatic timer, and that all other lightbulbs had been loosened. She cursed being hoodwinked yet again.

Eventually, the CSU team headed down the alley after the work had been completed and the guesthouse secured. McCallister began her walk back to the car, feeling both frustration and exuberance. She thought of Alexander Sinclair in some cell across town, and she tried to determine if any guilt tied itself to the image in her mind. She replayed the venomous words Alexander had spewed in the interrogation room, and she felt none. She listed the evidence in which the DA put such stock, and she felt none. She remembered Hastings' description of how Faraday had probably suffered, and she felt none. The sudden side road in the investigation changed little regarding the case. She tried to let go.

The sight of Holly went a very long way to help with that task. She jumped out of the car as soon as she saw McCallister approaching. Right there under a streetlight in a conservative neighborhood, she embraced her and kissed her repeatedly. Then came the slap on the arm. "That was so stupid of you, Laura!" she reprimanded.

"It was, hon," McCallister said without defense. "I'm sorry. I lost my head. It will never happen again."

She swatted her arm again. "Your not losing your head again is about as likely as me never losing my panties again," she retorted as she slipped back into the car.

Claudia's head shot to Holly, her jaw dropping in the process. "Headless Girl Detective and the Case of the Missing Panties," she quipped. "I don't even want to think about it."

An hour later, Holly and McCallister were entwined and sleeping.

Eight hours later, McCallister was staring into the confused faces of Jansen and Jessop on the front step of the Faraday house. She had summoned them without explanation. Between sips of her coffee from Timmer's, she filled them in on what had happened since the infamous plane to Maine took off without them.

"So I want everything catalogued in English," she eventually concluded. "Everything always seems to come back to these orchids, so let's just get a handle on what he's got. The code from the book in the guesthouse could easily point to an orchid that holds some clue. A clue to what, that's another question."

Jessop opened the front door and then quickly jotted their names and the time into the crime scene logbook. McCallister surrendered her coffee to the front step, and they all went into the house.

She made a beeline for the sitting room to make sure she kept her promise to Dr. Spangler before he arrived. She put the photograph of the rare orchid on an end table. Then, she walked to Holly's painting and transcribed the code, "CatIF.07.98.317," that Holly had included at Frederick's direction. She knew it differed in length from the other one, but she trusted that Spangler would understand.

When the botanist and his students arrived, McCallister had them put on protective garments, and then she led them to Faraday's command center in the greenhouse. She explained what she needed, knowing full well that Spangler had already briefed them. The fact that he had became very apparent when his three students moved into quick action. The young woman took charge of a notebook that would hold all of Faraday's codes with an understandable explanation to follow, once the specified orchid was found. The two young men held sticky notes and pens. They were tasked with determining locations, affixing an identification tag to each plant, and then feeding the location back to the young woman. It seemed confusing to McCallister, but the whole concept of the catalogue did as well. She would simply have to trust.

"Before you guys get totally lost in this, I'd like to start with these two," she said, handing Spangler the paper with the two codes that baffled her.

"Let's back up a step, Detective, so you understand," he recommended. He grabbed a piece of paper and motioned for McCallister to stand next to him by the bench. He proceeded to draw four lines down the paper.

"The first column is the species and subspecies information; that's the first part of the code with the letters. The second column is for the next two sets of numbers; this becomes his birth date for the plant. Third is the lot number, which denotes staging number and position. The last one, which some of them won't have, is for any crossings he did between plants." He looked to McCallister for some sign that she understood, but she was completely void.

"I'm sorry," she said. "I'm really not a stupid person, but this just confounds me."

"I warned you that his system wasn't revolutionary," he said with a laugh. "In fact, it's downright rudimentary, but it worked for him." He flapped McCallister's piece of paper and suggested. "Let's do one together, and see if it makes sense that way." He started with the one from the guesthouse.

McCallister leaned in and read the code again, "ChaMys.04.79.425. x58x66."

"The letters basically indicate the name of the flower ... three letters from species and three from subtype. He's got the birth date as April 1979. The 425 means that the plant is on the 4th staging in the 25th position. The Xs with numbers mean that the plant is a cross between 58 and 66, which we'll find on his tags up here, if we care to understand the cross."

McCallister scratched her head and laughed, feeling no more enlightened and no less frustrated. "That is utter nonsense to me," she admitted with a chuckle. "But if it makes sense to you, then I'm really glad you're here. What did make sense to me, though, was the location. That's really what I want to know. Can we find this one?"

Spangler nodded and looked to one of the young men. "James, it's 425. Can you get it for her?"

McCallister interjected, "I'd rather we not touch it, just in case there's evidence. But, if you lead the way, James, I will gladly follow."

He nodded, and she made her way with him. Abruptly, he stopped and turned to the doctor. He contorted his face and said, "Dr. Spangler, there are only three stagings."

Spangler laughed. "See, Detective, even a botanist can get screwed up by his system. Don't feel bad." Everyone laughed, and then he suggested, "Let's try the other one, since it at least looked simpler." He grabbed the paper and instructed James, "Cat IF, from July of 1998, staging 3, number 17."

James and McCallister headed to the last staging. She watched as he counted positions. He went to a plant, looked to its tag, and confirmed, "I have it. It's a Cattleya Irene Finney."

"Good work, James!" Spangler yelled. "And bravo to me for getting one right." He laughed and looked again to the other code.

McCallister approached the plant. It looked exactly like the one that Holly had painted. She quickly put on a pair of gloves and then lifted the pot to look under it. She was unsure what she was looking for but did not want to risk overlooking anything. Finding nothing, she slowly spun the pot, examining as she went. Looking on the back of the plant stick, she saw the words, "For Holly Crawford." She felt satisfied that the code merely pointed to the orchid he had Holly paint. The system made a bit more sense to her. She headed back to Spangler.

"I'm sorry about this other code," he rued. "Either I'm missing something, or Faraday made a mistake. If I figure it out, I'll let you know. In the meantime, take your paper back so it doesn't get mixed in with what we are about to do."

"And you guys have loads of fun with what you are about to do!" she joked. "I'll be in the study if you need anything … or find anything." She turned to leave, but Spangler immediately stopped her.

He explained that Faraday's orchids had gone days without care. "Would it be okay if we at least watered them? He has some remarkable plants here. It would be a shame if— Oh, did you get to see the sixty-year-old plant with its bloom, Detective?" He looked to his students. "You guys will love it!"

They all followed him to the third staging. He pointed—to the exact place McCallister remembered finding the green bottle of poison. "It was here," Spangler said. "He must have moved it. Let me look." He sped up and down the aisles in search of the rare plant. Unable to find it, he asked if it had been removed during the investigation. "The bloom was orange," he offered. "A brilliant and beautiful orange."

McCallister believed there would have been no reason for anyone to remove a plant. She also did not remember seeing it during her initial examination of the greenhouse. "I'll get the crime scene photos. If it was here when we arrived, it will be in the pictures," she assured him.

"It's rare," Spangler added with urgency. "It could fetch thousands of dollars, but more so, its cells for cloning are truly invaluable!"

With a mission in mind, McCallister left Dr. Spangler and his students to their work. She told them that they could water the plants as long as they were extremely careful.

She caught up with Jansen and asked him to get someone from the station to bring the crime scene photos. Then, she headed into the sitting room and stared at Holly's painting. In the grand scheme of things, the code Holly had painted meant nothing, and yet, it helped McCallister somewhat understand Faraday's reverse Dewey.

Her cell phone rang, and she answered it to learn from the lab that the only fingerprints found in the guesthouse belonged to Faraday.

Frederick *was* Faraday. But, what did that have to do with anything other than a pen name on an article and the commissioning of a painting? Then she reasoned that if Frederick was Faraday, searching the guesthouse was no different from searching the main house. Each belonged to the victim.

# Chapter 9

When she arrived at the guesthouse, she found Kate staked out in the alley. "You're snooping!" McCallister accused.

"I am not," she adamantly defended. "I'm doing my job. I'm hanging out waiting for crumbs from you."

"Yes, but you only know to be here because of what I told you."

"I did not submit an article today," she defended more loudly. "I told you to trust me. I kept my word." She smiled and dared ask, "But do you have anything for me that I can tell the world?"

"Not a thing," she said. "Not a damn thing. I know I'm missing something right in front of my face."

"Will you at least tell me what happened here last night?" Kate asked, obviously frustrated that McCallister had successfully deflected all questions on the ride home the night prior. "I'm dying to know what the body actually turned out to be and if you found this Frederick guy. I'm still laying odds that he did it and not the sister."

She laughed, wanting desperately to tell her and at the same time not wanting to blur the line between police and press, private and public. "Let's have a smoke," she said.

They moved further down the alley. Douglas Penning's basset hound saw them and began barking so they quickly moved in the opposite direction. There, they each lit a cigarette.

"I wish you weren't a reporter, Kate," McCallister finally said.

"Well, if you can magically stop being a detective and turn into an unnamed source, why the hell can't I magically go from reporter to listener?" she proposed. "In all these years, I've never betrayed your trust. Plus, I don't do the 'out for blood' like the rest."

McCallister thought for a moment and decided to risk it. She needed to bounce things off someone further removed from the investigation. If there was truly something in front of her face, everyone was missing it, not just her.

"Okay, listener," she finally said. "Thaddeus A. Frederick is Tobias A. Faraday. That's why no one has ever seen Frederick. He doesn't exist."

Kate's jaw dropped, and her eyes widened. "Holy shit!" she exclaimed. "Why the hell didn't I think of that?"

"Why the hell didn't *I* think of that?" McCallister countered.

"Yes, but I just did a whole piece on the Faradays the day he was found murdered. Family history stuff," she explained. "His father's name was Frederick. His grandfather's name was Thaddeus. His middle initial comes from his mother's maiden name of Albert. That sneaky old man! What the hell was he hiding?"

"If I knew that, do you think I'd be huddled in the alley smoking cigarettes with a listener-slash-reporter?" she said. "He wrote that article … so it was a pen name. He used the name to commission Holly to paint a picture of an orchid for him. That's all I know."

"Holly?" she gasped. "How the hell does Holly fit into this?"

McCallister explained about the painting and the code, adamantly maintaining that it seemed a mere coincidence. Kate reluctantly agreed and then made the offer to check on what else he might have written under the pen name of T. A. Frederick. She headed to her car and tore away.

McCallister let herself into the guesthouse. Feeling confident that drawers could be pulled and doors could be opened, she searched the residence. Again, she came up empty-handed.

She headed back to the main house, and as she rounded the front corner, she nearly ran into Captain Greeley.

"Why if it isn't Detective Laura McCallister!" he wailed. "Why the hell aren't you in Maine?"

"Oh, hi, Cap," she said, plastering a smile of innocence on her face. "Fancy meeting you here."

"You damn well better be on the clock," he said. "And you damn well better fill me in on everything."

She filled him in—not that she had a choice.

He absorbed it all and then said, "This is crazy, Laura. He's messing with you. He's setting you up for something." He paused to think. "He knows procedure, Laura, which means he knows cops. He knows you. How does he know procedure? How does a seventy-three-year-old man know how to mess with cops? And why the hell would he? He was murdered, and suddenly the lights start coming on in the guesthouse, which is loaded with his prints only, which just happens to contain a fake body, which just happens to give you probable cause to enter, which just happens to put you onto some alias he was using." He put his hands on her shoulders. "Do you see what's in front of your face right now?"

She was indeed starting to see, and it made the gnawing knot pull so tight that it hurt.

Greeley displayed a large envelope to her. "I'm delivering the crime scene photos." When she reached for them, he pulled them back. "I'm also delivering a warning. You get so caught up in keeping honorable promises you make to victims that sometimes you lose sight of everything else. Yes, he's a victim, but if he's messing with you, with us, then he's got some malice inside as well. Quit looking into his eyes, Laura!" He flapped the envelope in the air. "I'll put Phil on this." He began to walk away, and then he stopped abruptly and turned to face her. "Since when do let *anybody* mess with you?" He glared at her and then resumed his quest to find Jansen.

Sufficiently castigated, she felt the stiffening of her spine as she allowed her anger to surface. Why the hell was he messing with her? How the hell did he know she would be there in order to be messed with? How did he know procedure?

She sped back to the guesthouse, this time pulling and shaking everything she could get her hands on. "Faraday, what the hell are doing?" she yelled as she went through the house. "How the hell did you know to do this? How did you know cops would be here? How did you know we'd need probable cause?"

She reasoned that he could not have arranged this all after he had drunk the poison, after it dawned on him that his sister had taken action to kill him. She further reasoned that his journal indicated his fear of his sister killing him. Maybe he had put this all in place, knowing the inevitable was coming. Alexandra had to have done it; she possessed more than enough hatred for him, and she wanted the money. She had motive with more than enough to spare. If he knew so much about procedure and cops, why hadn't he gone to the cops if he was convinced she was going to kill him? Why ask the cops for help after the fact? "What the hell are you doing, Faraday?" she yelled.

She pulled the bedspread and the sheets from the bed. She held the mattress high to see whether it hid anything. As she flung it to the side of the room, her foot banged into something under the bed. Without the humility that usually brings someone to that position, she got to her knees. She looked under the bed to discover pile after pile of leather-bound journals, all bearing "TAF" on the cover. She shook her head, "I don't have time so sit and read every thought you had for the last eon, Faraday. If that's what you expect, it isn't going to happen. What the hell are you—"

Her cell phone rang. The lab called to let her know that the substance found in the guesthouse contained the blood of Tobias Faraday. She disconnected without even a thank-you and dashed to the bathroom. A fake body in a pool of Faraday's blood. "So what, Faraday, you symbolically killed Thaddeus Frederick? Did that make you feel like a big man? Did you make-believe kill yourself so that—" McCallister froze. "Jesus f-ing Christ!"

Her head suddenly felt as though it was fifteen feet wide, like she could see a thought drifting by in slow motion until it disappeared out of sight. Then another would float by. Pieces. Disjointed pieces. They were easier to see as they floated, instead of when they were smashed into a tight big package. An altered will. An argument. A scratch. Poison. A dead man. A fake dead man. Codes. Riddles. Secrets.

If he knew procedure, did he know enough to commit the perfect crime—with himself as the victim and his sister as the killer? Did he know enough to become both the murdered and the murderer?

"I'm smarter than you, Faraday!" she shouted into the ether. "I know enough. Watch me!"

She headed back to the main house, this time nearly colliding with Jessop as they both rounded the corner. "We need a goddamn traffic light here!" she spat with an angry tone.

Jessop looked at her sheepishly. "Um, I'm making a run for lunch," he carefully began. "The doc said his kids are starving and need a break. He suggested a picnic on the front lawn. His treat. Can I get you anything?"

She faked a smile at him as she sensed a level of discomfort much higher than what she normally produced. "No, thank you, Jessop." She smiled again. "I'd sell my soul for a huge cup of coffee though."

He grinned at her. "You've got it, Detective."

Several minutes later, she eased into Faraday's chair in his study and put her feet up. She tilted back. "I know more than you, Faraday. I know procedure. I know about the perfect crime and that there is no such thing. From your chair here, I can get in your head. Watch me."

She scanned the room and speculated. She stared at the bookshelves: alphabetical by title. She watched the sun streaming though the windows: cleaned every Thursday. She looked to the antique lamp on the desk: appraised yearly. She slid her finger over the cigar box—Cubans smuggled in for a premium price but rarely smoked. She ran her eyes up and down the two stacks of mystery magazines—sorted by issue number. She glanced between two paintings on opposite walls: rotated every six months to minimize light burn. She looked to the papers and the penholder: stationer every other Thursday.

Suddenly, Jansen was at the door. A boastful grin nearly distorted his features. "Can I interrupt?" he asked. She nodded, and he began, "Cap put me on the crime scene photos. There was no orange flower when our photos were taken. I was first officer on the scene. No one went in until I secured it. Nothing in the logbook indicates an orchid was taken. So..." He paused to smile.

And it was contagious. Whatever he had to say pleased him to no end. McCallister had no choice but to smile right along with him.

"The doc helped me describe the thing, and I went to the station and started checking auction sites on the Web. Believe it or not, I found it, complete with a picture." He stopped to laugh. "Some criminals are so stupid, huh?"

She was laughing now and nodding her head in complete agreement.

"Anyway," he continued, "the seller wanted $2,500 for it. I contacted him privately and offered $5,000 if he'd pull the item and meet me right away. He agreed to meet me this afternoon. I quick looked at the other items he's selling, and there is a lot! I've got somebody cross-referencing as we speak."

He was full-blown laughing now, as was McCallister. "So..." he said again. "I was wondering if you'd like to take a ride with me over to Michael Endicott's house. Yes, the idiot gave me his name and address! A couple of keystrokes later, bingo! I figured out he's the husband of Faraday's housekeeper. She must have known about the orchid from Faraday and then called her husband before she even called 911 to report Faraday dead."

That last bit of information made the laughter dissipate instantly. McCallister quickly moved to salvage the mood. "That is so amazing, Jansen. I am proud of you! What incredibly good and fast work!"

"So do you want to go?"

"No," she said. "You enjoy your moment of glory for good sleuthing without bossy old me there to take over." She started smiling again, which got Jansen going as well. "Take Jessop with you and see if the wife cares to change her statement before or after her little trip downtown."

Then Jessop entered. He handed her the biggest cup of coffee she had ever seen. "Wow!" she exclaimed. "I can take a bath in this! Thank you! But, I can't be a bad cop and drink it in a crime scene. Can I, guys?"

"I guess you'll have to picnic with us on the front lawn with the doc and his kids," Jessop said with a grin.

She joined them all in the front of the house. They feasted on subs, chips, and sodas. It truly seemed picnic-like, not as if a crime scene loomed right behind them, hoarding its secrets. Neighbors passed by, trying to spy a look without being obvious.

McCallister took a spot on the front lawn near the talkative students.

"How are you guys doing in there? Better than I'd do, I hope"

The young woman remarked, "I have never seen so many orchids in all my life!"

McCallister chuckled to herself, always finding it humorous when a young person tried to emphasis something with their short life as the exclamation point. It was like the proverbial fish story. She looked at Spangler and asked, "Have you found any other clues with mistakes like the one I have?"

He shook his head while he finished chewing and swallowing. "No, I haven't," he finally said. "For the life of me, I can't figure out what he meant. I think he had to have made a simple mistake. Maybe when we finish, there'll be an extra plant, and then we'll know exactly what he meant."

One of the young men dared, "I can't figure out why he'd use a system like this. It seems insane. Why not just write what he meant? A small code on a plant stick makes sense, but not on all those notes on the wall." He shook his head and exhaled loudly through his nose.

"Maybe he wanted it to be difficult," James suggested.

"You mean to keep code-challenged people like me from finding something?" McCallister proposed. "CFBR6" ran through her mind. That seemed such child's play to her, and yet, she knew that not one of them there would think Chinese food. That was the point: It was private communication between people who understood the cryptic language. Two lovers. An orchidist and a botanist. A teacher and a student. Had Faraday figured her as someone who could decode the line in the journal from the guesthouse? Did he think just because someone could be a detective they could also crack a code? A mystery, a riddle, a puzzle—maybe, but not codes. His reverse Dewey made no sense to her.

She remembered the 'old days' before computers took over. She'd go the library with an author and title, pull the skinny drawer from the card catalogue, and end up with the book's exact position on the seemingly endless shelves. She even knew that the Agatha Christie books she craved sported an 813 on the spine. It baffled her to think of walking in with an 813 and coming out with Miss Marple in tow. Faraday may have known cops and procedure, but he didn't know enough to speak her language.

"Ah, but he did! Mr. Probable Cause!" she suddenly yelled, shooting to a standing position and spilling coffee in the process.

Her declaration caused all conversation to cease and all eyes to turn to her.

"What did you say, Detective?" Spangler asked.

She apologized for her outburst and moved away from the picnickers. She lit a cigarette. Titling her head back on exhale, she looked to the perfectly blue sky and felt the warming sun on her face. She took a swig from the bathtub-sized coffee cup. And she thought some more.

He hadn't named the fake dead body some exotic orchid name, leaving her to learn that it produced blood-red flowers and that its Latin name meant "probable cause." He had spoken her language. Plain and simple.

She grabbed the paper from her pocket and stared at the code again: *ChaMys.04.79.425.x58x66.* What did that mean if he had written it in her language?

Reverse Dewey: code leads to name … position leads to name. Reverse the reverse Dewey: name leads to position. Her mind scrambled to recall Spangler's explanation of the confounding system. *Partial names. Date. Position. Cross.* She repeated the four terms over and over in her mind. Then, she chanted what each one meant. *Cha Mys. April 1979. Staging 4, position 25. Cross 58 with 66.*

"Position leads to name," she whispered. "But the position doesn't exist." At least not in the greenhouse. She thought of police codes, something in her own language. There wasn't a 425, not in Granton anyway. Code 4, however, meant that no further assistance was required, and that made her laugh. She did need assistance and plenty of it.

*Miss Marple, where are you?* she joked to herself.

*I'm at 813, Detective.*

*Well, go to 425, and tell me what you see!*

*I don't see anything, Detective. It's a mystery to me.*

That made her laugh, too, but it also turned on a flood lamp in her mind. White, hot light illuminated the darkest corners. She let out a loud roll of laughter. Immediately, she looked to the picnickers, all staring at her again as though she teetered on a psychiatric borderline. "I am so slow sometimes!" she shouted to them. She threw her cigarette into the street and then stooped to put her coffee cup on the sidewalk. Eagerly, she spun on her heels and made a mad dash to Faraday's study.

"Watch me, Faraday!" she yelled upon entry. She approached the tower of *Chalkline Mysteries.* "Cha Mys, Faraday. Title gets position. Position gets title. And I get you."

She scanned the spines with a squinting eye, smiling broadly when she finally spied "#425." Carefully she pulled it from the tottering tower. Issue 425 bore the date of April 1979. The fold of a piece of paper barely peeked out from the small magazine. She opened to the page, knowing full well that she'd find a 58 there. Trusting the sudden return of her instincts, she mindfully flipped to the opposite half of the paper. Indeed, the paper enfolded pages 58 through 66. "I got you, Faraday!" she shouted.

She removed the piece of paper that had successfully completed its mission. Respectfully, she unfolded it and read the first line on the page, "Detective Laura McCallister, I presume."

# Chapter 10

McCallister's mind seemed to split itself in two. There was the one side that told her she should be disturbed by the man's presumption. What else had he presumed? Why was this personal? The other side, though, proved much louder. She felt the thrill of victory, the sense that she had finally thrown a powerful punch in her one-on-one death match with deception. Maybe it was simply the same kind of paradox she had recognized when talking with Greeley. *Don't mess with me, but if you do, at least be a formidable opponent.*

She read the salutation again, and then she said, "I got you, Faraday, and now you got me. Touché."

She took the magazine and the letter and scurried to Faraday's seat behind the desk. She propped up her feet and readied herself to devour what this time she had truly earned.

*Detective Laura McCallister, I presume.*

*I trust that you have gotten this far by sleuth and not ransack. Well done.*

*I also trust that you are angry with me. The very idea saddens me greatly, but at the same time, I cannot blame you. My hands are cold from death, and yet, they have stayed clenched to your shoulders, trying to direct you where I need you to go. The chill will leave you soon. It is almost done.*

*First of all, let me tell you what I suspect you need to hear most of all. Yes, this is personal, but only because I need your help, not because I suffer from some deviant obsession. My own privacy is precious to me, and*

I would not and did not invade yours.

Many times, I have seen your name in the paper— the detective who solves the mysteries in this sleepy little city that sometimes awakens in mid-nightmare. This is how I came to know you. This is how I came to respect your skill.

I met you only once with intent. Rather, Thaddeus A. Frederick made a point of meeting you. As him and with his enviable courage, I attended a self-defense workshop that you put on for seniors in the community. I just wanted to put a face and a voice to your name. Learning something to help this old man defend himself, well, that didn't hurt either. That is all.

Unintentionally, I spied you on many a Saturday morning in the front window at Timmer's Book 'n Bean. Coffee and a Christie. That is how I came to know your love of reading mysteries, your love of books. One of my own guilty pleasures, as well, and my only reason for allowing brave Thaddeus to slip into Timmer's.

Also unintentionally, I saw you at an art show in City Square. That is how I learned of Holly and her exceptional talent. I saw how the two of you looked at each other. Your love for each other was palpable, even from my distance. I deeply regret that my life has come to a close without ever having felt that way. Cherish what you have, Detective!

And then, there is the painting, which I would wager is what bothers you the most in my little game. Again, there is nothing that I must confess. I only saw Holly from a distance on the one occasion just mentioned. When she walked you to the elevator, I took one of her business cards. Then, I learned of her work by visiting the gallery. Her paintings are beautiful, and I selfishly wanted one of my own. I commissioned who you love the most in your life to paint what I loved the most in mine. Again, I hid behind Thaddeus in order to do it, and I must admit that I rudely denied Holly's request to speak with me about the details she needed—so that I did not cross a line, your line, because, as I indicated, I respect you.

*While this letter doesn't answer all of your questions, I must end this one here because of such respect. You are a fine detective, and you will not think twice about placing this letter into an evidence bag or discussing it in open court. I stop here because I __want__ you to think twice. The evidence I have just given exposes you far more than me. That is not fair; that is not respect. I will give you everything you need to know regarding your investigation, but at this moment in time, I have given you nothing crucial.*

*This letter does not need to be in evidence if you do not want it there. It is your privacy at risk here, not mine.*

*Fold it, put it in your pocket, and leave with it, if you will. Only you and I will know, and trust me, the cadaver I am now will not tell a soul.*

*Tobias A. Faraday*

"Shit!" she yelled with a fist to the desk.

He did indeed know how to speak her language. He did indeed know how to mess with her because he identified what was truly important in her life. And yet, he made a point of not crossing lines, acquiring only information that anyone in Granton could discover by simply paying attention.

And he had not messed with Holly. Above all, that relieved her, and she suddenly allowed herself to feel what she had managed to hold back from the moment she saw Holly's painting in the sitting room. Tears rose in her throat. While she would not and could not shed them at that juncture, merely acknowledging them eased a great burden.

And the 'out' he had given her—that one proved more difficult for her to grapple with. Yes, he had messed with her, but at the same time, he gave her a way to protect herself. And now—as much as she resisted, she was doing what Greeley told her not to do: She again peered into his cloudy eyes.

Interrupting that unsettling gaze, McCallister's cell phone made its presence known. She answered it to hear the results of Kate's foray into the literary world of T. A. Frederick. She said she spoke with the editor for *American Orchidist Association Magazine* and learned that Frederick had written four articles for them over the past years, all of which pertained to Tobias Faraday. The editor indicated that Faraday's appeal came not so much for his vast knowledge but more for the myth behind him ... that most in the orchid community knew *of* him, but no one actually knew him. She said the editor had been most eager for Frederick's last article, even to the point of helping him get it done, as he had told her that Faraday was dying,

"How did he know, Laura?" Kate asked, her voice near the begging stage. "*Was* he dying of something? Or did he know he was going to be murdered?"

McCallister told her she didn't know, and that was not an untruth. She didn't know, and speculation at that point, especially the audible kind, would not help her. Following him through his own denouement would—hopefully.

Kate gave McCallister the magazine editor's name and phone number. McCallister wagered that one quick call would pinpoint who the middle-aged woman was that the neighbors had seen visiting the guesthouse. She assured Kate that if she learned anything newsworthy, she'd let her know. "Until then," she said, "I'm afraid you're back to slinking around looking for crumbs."

She ended that call and could not help but speculate, or at least pose the question that required speculation. How did he know he was about to become a cadaver who could "not tell a soul"? She would need to leave his icy hands on her shoulders for a while longer, letting him steer her to where he was sure she needed to go.

She grabbed the *Chalkline Mysteries* magazine and flipped to page fifty-eight. "Sound Reasoning by T. A. Frederick," that page began. She quickly flipped to the front cover, just to reaffirm the day of April 1979 and to fathom that Frederick's existence suddenly spanned decades.

Eagerly, she began to read, only to be stopped by the text message tone on her phone. "Dinner 6:00? I love you. I miss you." She looked to her watch, realizing that it was going on one-thirty. She thumbed, "Yes, 6. I love and miss you, too. Very much." After sending it, she returned to "Sound Reasoning," knowing that she could certainly use a dose of that.

## Sound Reasoning by T. A. Frederick

Albert Regis lay on his bed, desperately pressing his hands over his ears to blot out the horrid sound.

He remembered waking the day prior; how different it had been. Summer vacation mornings afforded him the luxury of lingering in bed to plan his wide-open day. A ride to town on his bike? Begging the neighbor man to take him driving as his temps burned a hole in his back pocket? Maybe fishing. Maybe read a book. Maybe a swim in the pond. Maybe nothing but a boring movie on television. For a fifteen-year-old boy, the possibilities were endless, and Albert liked to ponder them all.

He squeezed his hands tighter to his head, but he still heard it. He flipped to his stomach and frantically brought his pillow over his head. Again, he pressed as hard as he could to keep the sound from getting inside him. The auditory invasion made him sick to his stomach; he wanted to vomit. In his mind, he saw his mouth become like a fire hose, propelling his acidic bile with immense pressure until it covered everything he disdained.

*No one should have to hear this,* he screamed inside, trying to make his inner voice louder than what reverberated outside his skull. But again, it was to no avail. He imagined tiny little fragments of sound marching up his body, running single-file to his ears and then into his defenseless brain—assembling, falling into line, gathering, congregating until there were enough of them to create one ghastly noise. He compressed his pillow tighter to his head.

And then there was silence.

He envisioned the boy wiping his sister's spit off his mouth. Maybe he would smile at her as he stood to pull up his jeans. Maybe he would say, "See you tomorrow," over the zipping sound he made. Whatever he did, Albert could only imagine with great disgust. But, what he did know for certain was that next, the boy would make his way to the bedroom window, slink down the trellis, and steal off out of sight.

And what was she doing in there now, the slut? Those imaginings he always refused to entertain.

She did this more times than he could count. As soon as he heard his parents close the front door to leave for work, he began the vigil. His ears would switch between car door slams and listening for feet on the trellis … engines starting and feet on the trellis … distant engine sound and feet on the trellis. When he could no longer hear his parents' engines in the distance, he concentrated solely on the trellis. If he heard feet and hands clawing their way up, he'd wait for the horrid sound that was sure to follow, the sound no brother should have to hear. Then, he'd close his ears.

Sometimes it was a low-voiced boy. Sometimes it was a high-pitched boy. Sometimes it was the one who laughed. Sometimes, the silent one. She had a parade of them. Some mornings she was grand marshal. Some mornings no one marched to her beat. The inconsistency drove him mad. If no sound came within twenty minutes after his parents left, he knew it was safe.

Today was not safe.

He got up and crept down the hall, past her now-quiet room. He snuck into the bathroom and turned on the faucets in the shower until the water neared scalding. Then, as he had done on every other occasion, he burned the intrusive sound off his body. He'd visualize the tiny little fragments of sound that hadn't made it to the assembly in time ... swirling at the drain, pulled into the vortex, banished.

With as much stealth, Albert exited the bathroom and tiptoed down the stairs. He walked into the kitchen, swiping the note his mother always left on the counter. The paper was divided into two columns. He owned half, his sister, the other. Chores for the day ran down the columns. Today he was expected to water the garden and straighten up the shed. She, on the other hand, was to dust the living room, mop the kitchen, and peel potatoes for dinner. Never did her column say, "Screw the boy du jour."

Frequently he wondered what they'd think if they knew. Oftentimes, he wanted to tell them ... just to make the sound stop. A couple of times, he had even opened his mouth to do just that, but he stopped in panic before a word even had a chance to form. He was torn. As sickened as he was by her disregard for what was right, he did not want to lessen her in the eyes of his parents. He could hate her and love her at the same time. This confused him, but he hadn't been able to stop it—no matter how hard he tried.

By telling, he also did not want to lessen himself in the eyes of his parents. Good boys didn't think such things, much less say them aloud. If they didn't believe him, if they didn't see the dire necessity in ripping the trellis from the wall, they would think he was as twisted as the morning glory vines clinging to it. But, he knew he wasn't twisted. He knew he could never be like her, that he would never be like her. He would never need to wipe someone's spit off his mouth because he knew he could never do it without thinking of her.

He looked to the bottom of his mother's note. "I love you. Mom," it always read, and it always grabbed him by the scruff of the neck to ensure his silence.

He quietly grabbed a bowl from the cupboard and then collected the cereal, a spoon, and the milk carton. He ate as quickly as he could and then snuck back upstairs before she arose.

In his room, he threw on shorts, a T-shirt, and tennis shoes. Then he went to his dresser. Although his door was closed, he scanned the room to make sure he was completely alone. He clutched the wooden cigar box his father had given him. Again, he looked around the room before removing the stacks of baseball cards that rested inside. After setting them safely on his dresser, his hand went into the box, pushed on the far corner to jimmy the felt-covered board, and withdrew the fake bottom. There was his secret, his sin: a single cigarette sat. He helped it make its way from the cigar box to the pocket of his T-shirt. He replaced the bottom and the baseball cards.

No longer concerned about rousing her, he sped out of the house and made a beeline for the shed.

He opened the shed's door, assessing the extent of the work involved in straightening up. It didn't seem that big a deal, so he quickly did what was expected of him. He put the garden tools in their proper places. He moved the gas can where it belonged by the lawnmower, and he closed the box of plant food that someone had left open. He brushed the potting soil off the workbench and then quickly gave the area a sweep.

With his work done in record time, he neared the bag of charcoal for his father's grill. He grabbed the lighter and snuck out to the back of the shed. With his spine to the wall, he stretched out and retrieved the cigarette from his pocket. Knowing it had to last until he could swipe another from the neighbor man's house, he took his time both lighting it and smoking it. The sensation of drawing in the smoke and holding the cigarette between his fingers made him feel manly, strong. Ofttimes he figured he could do just about anything with one clutched between his two fingers. He relaxed and let the morning's stress float away in a whirl of white smoke.

Shattering the mood, she suddenly towered over him. As she leered down at him, she proclaimed, "I knew you were smoking! It took me a while to catch you, but now I have you. I'm telling." She let out a wicked laugh.

"You can't tell!" he yelled. "They'll kill me."

"Well, then," she said, "maybe we can make a deal. All my chores for the rest of the summer."

"Bull!" he spat back at her. "I've got worse things on you. If you tell on me, I'll tell on you. What you do is a lot worse than having one stupid cigarette." He glared into her smiling, arrogant face. "I know what you do in the morning after they leave. I can hear you, and it makes me sick. You make me sick."

She just laughed. "Oh, listening to your little sister, are you? You pervert! You're just jealous."

"How could I possibly be jealous of that?" he challenged, clutching the bare remainder of his cigarette like a man. "They don't care about you! They're using you."

"And what makes you think I'm not using them?" she countered. "Guys are all the same. A little yank in the right place, and they'll do whatever I want."

With a fire-red face, he defended, "I'm not like that! I'll never be like that."

"You're right, dear brother. You'll never be like that because you'll never find anyone willing to yank." She laughed manically, and it slowly turned into tiny little fragments of sound crawling on his body in search of his ears. She taunted, "You'll just have to be happy with how Mommy and Daddy dote over their precious little boy. It's all you'll ever have."

He moved his hands to cover his ears, dropping the spent cigarette butt as he did so. He squeezed his head until it felt as though it would burst, like an explosion of glass, each shard reflecting her laughing face and bouncing the sound back at him. He squeezed even harder and started rocking in place. "At least they love me! At least they love me!" he chanted.

* * * * *

She peeled the potatoes like a good girl. Her mother would be proud.

Nearly depleted, the ten-pound bag slumped next to the sink.

With each flick of her wrist, the peeler made a scraping sound, followed by a tiny little clink as the blade swung back into position. She concentrated on the clink. The scrape was easy to hear. The clink took discernment and a careful ear. But, the effort was well rewarded; it drowned out that horrid morning sound still echoing in her skull, floating there like whirls of black, black smoke.

Suddenly, the door burst open, and her mother shrieked, "What happened to the shed? It's gone—it's smoldering! What happened? Are you okay? Where is Albert?"

She screamed so loud that it made it difficult for her to concentrate on the clink. She needed the clink.

"Where is Albert?" her mother screamed.

Needing to shut her up so she could hear the clink, she said, "He's out by the shed smoking."

*Scrape. Clink. Scrape. Clink...*

"Holy shit!" McCallister gasped, flipping once more to the cover to see the date: April 1979.

# Chapter 11

On any other occasion, McCallister would have enjoyed the story. She would have pondered the possibilities, thought about the characters, perhaps read it again in search of nuances. This occasion, this story, however, proved sorely different: a now-deceased man killed by his sister had penned a story decades ago about a tormented boy and his unstable sister. She realized it was fiction, and yet, the prophetic nature of it caused her mind to reason that the author, Frederick/Faraday, had probably written from a place of understanding. But, did it stem from an understanding he gleaned as he wrote it or from things he remembered from his childhood? She reasoned that it did not matter. It offered no further proof of what had happened in this house three days ago; it was merely a glimpse into the minds of two fictional characters. Motivations and fears—supportive of the conclusions, maybe, but still fiction, pure and not so simple.

Her eyes scanned the story again. She smiled to herself.

With the utmost confidence, McCallister ran her finger along the wooden cigar box on the desk. She wondered if Faraday's father had really given it to him when he was young and if it truly had stowed his boyhood secrets. She would have bet her life that if it didn't then, it did now.

She carefully removed the lid from the box, the strong scent of cigars rapidly expanding in the room. Imagining baseball cards instead of cigars, she removed the contents and placed them on the desk. Remembering what the fictional Albert had done, she inserted her hand, fiddled with the bottom corner, and pulled out the felt panel. She peered in to find one lone cigarette, a bright yellow and blue pack of baseball cards, and a folded sheet of paper. Oddly, she took the pack of baseball cards first, finding it unopened, ridges indicating that even the stick of bubble gum, albeit shattered, still resided within. She set it aside. The cigarette made her want her own, so she ignored it and instead grabbed the piece of paper.

Again, the first line read, "Detective Laura McCallister, I presume." She acknowledged that he had begun both letters in the same way, obviously in case the prior one had landed in her pocket for a hasty trip out the door. He was keeping his word. He was respecting her lines. He was protecting her—needlessly, but that did not devalue his intent.

"These are my secrets and sins, at least the ones that matter at the moment," the impeccable penmanship read.

_T. A. Frederick_: That name has been with me for many years, as you now know. I assure you it is not a separate part of my personality—no Jekyll and Hyde tale here. It is nothing more than a pseudonym. Speaking through someone else's pen or tongue allowed me to say what I was too fearful to say on my own. I found it truly amazing just how freeing it was to 'be' him. By simply putting on a wig and a mustache, I could be more of who I am, or maybe who I was supposed to have been if I had not let fear take over when I was young. He was my spine, and for that I am grateful, despite how dishonoring it is for me to have to admit it now.

_Albert Regis_: He is simply a fictional character, and yet, any novice writer is told to write what he knows, and so I did. I know the sounds that tormented him. I know the fears and the disgust. I know the foreboding in the assertion that I would always be alone, loved only by Mother and Father. And I know what it is like to love my sister no matter how I tried not to, no matter how many reasons she gave me to feel the contrary.

_Albert's Sister_: Again, she is simply a fictional character. She is a nameless one, because the name that belonged to her, I could not write, and yet, I could not bring myself to fictionalize it either. The sin of spinelessness again.

Throughout my entire life, _Alex_ has proven to be my ultimate mystery, but sadly, that mystery remained unsolvable to me. I have never been able to figure her out; thus, I have never been able to save her from herself. She is not happy; she has never been happy. And yes, I sensed her hatred of me since I was a little boy, and yes, I have always believed that she was quite capable of killing me—if I ever crossed a certain line. I just never knew

92

*where that line was—until recently when I stumbled on it.*

*Everything I have researched about her lifelong behaviors says that something unspeakable must have happened to her as a child. I thought endlessly on this. I analyzed everyone we knew as children. I asked Alex in a hundred different subtle ways. If someone abused her, I do not know about it. Is it possible, Detective, for someone 'simply' to be born abusive and vindictive? I do not know. My sin here is that I failed her as a brother. For this, I am acutely sorry.*

*I assume that while you are sitting here humoring an old man, Alex is sitting in a jail cell. That is what has to be. I am hoping beyond hope that the closeness of walls, the lack of freedom and control will show her what is truly important in this life before it is too late. Tell your DA that records probably still exist for the times when Mother and Father tried to get her help: Lincoln Shores, St. Michael's, Reed. Despite how Alex will tell you that they didn't love her, they did—without question. They tried to help. They paid good money to keep it quiet, too, so your DA must seek records for Christina Alexander. And Dorsey, if he is at all worth his salt, will try for an insanity defense, hopefully getting her transferred to a psychiatric facility when her bail is denied.*

*This must work, Detective. This is my very last shot.*

*Tobias A. Faraday*

McCallister set the paper down on the desk. "What was the line you crossed, Tobias?"

For the life of her, she could not imagine why he had just let this happen. Why wasn't he angry? Why hadn't he defended himself? Why didn't he see that getting help for himself before the fact might have resulted in her getting help? Did he really think hell's fire was the only salve for what he called his sin?

Three times, she scanned the letter, making sure she hadn't missed anything, a clue that would keep her on trail of the truth. She looked at the package of baseball cards, the lone cigarette, and the bottom of the cigar box. When it seemed a dead end, she went to the tower of *Chalkline Mysteries* and inspected them, looking for any with a paper stuck inside. Finding nothing, she did the same to the other stack of

*Watson's Enigma.* Nothing. Either he was appealing to her sleuth again, or the simple statement she had just read was all he thought she needed to know. Alexandra had a history, but that information helped both sides: the prosecution and the defense. He wanted her deemed insane so that she got the help she needed. Why hadn't he given all this information to Dorsey then so he could provide an adequate defense? Discovery would have eventually gotten the information to the DA. Why give it to a detective—one he said had skill—if her job was to establish guilt and not defend?

"Why the hell are you still stringing me along, Tobias? And why the hell aren't you angry?"

Suddenly, she felt glad that he had provided no further clues. Her head hurt with all the thoughts teeming in it. She imagined it bulging and retracting with the activity. She needed to stop the movement, to slow down. She needed to step back.

She grabbed her cell and punched in Kate's number. "Sutter, are you in the alley looking for crumbs?" she asked after the greeting. When she received affirmation, she said, "Light one for me. I'm on my way."

As she made her out of the house, she found Bartholomew at the front door. She asked what he was doing there, and he replied, "Jansen asked me to keep an eye on the scene while him and Jessop went to Endicott's."

She nodded to him and then went to stick her head into the greenhouse. "Any codes that don't fit?" she asked with both hope and dread. She did not want to resort to ransack after Faraday had commended her sleuth. She also knew that she would if it came to that.

"Everything's on the money so far, Detective," Spangler replied.

"If you find anything that begins with c-h-a-m-y-s or w-a-t-e-n-i, please let me know right away," she instructed and then hightailed it to the alley.

She laughed when she found Kate sitting on the alley's pavement, holding two lit cigarettes. "You know, Sutter," she said. "There aren't any crumbs back here. A lot of ashes, but no crumbs."

Kate joined the laughter. "Then where are the crumbs, Gretel?"

"Beats me, Hansel, but at the moment, I'm more concerned with making some ashes." She seized the longer of the two cigarettes Kate held and took a long, desperate drag. On exhale, she stretched her tense body like a cat that had just stepped in water. "Do you know where your colleagues are?" She was curious; sometimes the press found out things the cops couldn't. Knowing their guesses occasionally improved her own.

"They're in front of the station," Kate said. "Waiting for her to post

94

bail and slink away while they take pictures, I suppose."

"She won't get an initial hearing until Monday morning," McCallister informed her. "If you get busted for something big, never let it happen on a Friday."

Kate laughed. "I'll keep that in mind. Thanks for the advice, Detective."

They sat in silence for several minutes. Kate kept her eyes glued to McCallister. "Edgy" and "exhausted" were the adjectives she would choose if she were allowed to report her observations.

McCallister finally broke the silence. "So do you want to enjoy some of your weekend, or do you want me to ruin it more by giving you something to do?" she asked, extinguishing her cigarette and promptly lighting another.

Kate smiled and held out her coffee cup to McCallister. When it was quickly confiscated, she said, "Well, since your better half stole my better half to go fetch your luggage at the airport, I think I'd rather have something to do."

McCallister took a swig of coffee and told her about the two stacks of mystery magazines. "If I'm not mistaken, both those magazines date back to the forties," she said. "I have no idea how to do it, or even if they keep archives from that long ago, but I need to know about any stories written by T. A. Frederick. I just need issue numbers."

"Oh, is that all?" Kate rolled her eyes and grabbed the PDA from her pocket. "Does the Faraday house have Wi-Fi?"

McCallister laughed. "You are kidding, right? Paper and pen for this guy. I bet his phone is rotary dial."

"Yes, I was kidding." She began thumbing, and a couple of minutes later, she said, "*Chalkline* lists only current authors. ... Archives aren't searchable. Probably the same with the other. Give me a few."

As she waited, McCallister's eyes scanned the back of the Faraday house, half-expecting a trellis of morning glories to rise to a second-story window.

"Okay," Kate said. "I found a collector's site that has all the issues divided by years. ... Listing each author and story title for every issue. It'll take me a while, but I can do it."

McCallister rose and smiled at her. "Thanks, Sutter. And by the way, your better half should be home by six. At least mine will be. So take your little gadget and do that at home. I think I might call it a day as well." She glanced to her watch. "It's almost three. Go home." She handed the empty coffee cup to her and took delight in the dirty look it garnered.

Halfway back to the house, her cell rang. Jansen's eager voice said, "Detective, I've got Endicott at the station. I've got the orchid; it looks

95

okay. Plus, I've got something else you might be interested in. Can you come down?"

She told him she was headed in that direction anyway, that she would be there as soon as she sent the doctor and his kids home and locked up. She sped to the greenhouse, telling them that they could quit for the day. They agreed to meet the next afternoon at one. As they removed their protective garments at the front door, she asked about how to take care of the orchid until they could get it released from Property & Evidence.

"Give it a good drink in a sink," he instructed. "Until the bark looks dark and wet. Then get it to an east window. No direct sun. If you can't manage that, try to get it as close to fluorescent lights as possible." He stared directly into her eyes. "Please don't let anything happen to it."

Twenty minutes later, she walked into the squad room. Immediately, she noticed a tearful housekeeper sitting in a chair with a cop standing only feet away. McCallister knew that giving her the cold-shoulder would have sent the message just as clearly, but she couldn't resist. As she passed her, she said. "A dear man, isn't that what you called Faraday? Dear enough to let him lay in his own vomit for an extra hour, huh?"

She didn't bother to look for a reaction. Instead, she sped down the hall and entered the observation room. She peered through the mirror, watching Jansen and Jessop interrogate Michael Endicott.

"You might as well come clean," Jessop said. "Felony theft is a whole lot better than murder. Who's to say Faraday was dead when you got there? Who's to say you and your wife didn't kill him? You want your kid born in prison?"

"I know I'd rather be pegged as a thief than a murderer," Jansen added. "I'd feel safer in prison, too. Killing an old man doesn't generally get too much respect."

Endicott squirmed, as any 'normal' person in his position would. His face reddened, and he rubbed his hands roughly on his thighs. McCallister wondered why she had even been summoned; these two young cops were doing just fine. She looked to her watch, allowing the second hand to give them a full minute until he cracked.

"I didn't kill anybody!" Endicott yelled. "The paper said you already busted his sister."

"Maybe we got it wrong," Jansen said. "Maybe there's an innocent woman about to take the fall for what you and your wife did."

Jessop swatted Jansen's arm. "How pregnant did his wife say she was? Six months? Yep, she'll be in prison before she pops."

"I swear I didn't kill him!"

McCallister glanced to her watch, knowing full well that the next sentence out of his mouth would result in the clank of a cell door

96

closing.

"He was dead when Jenny got there. He was dead when I got there."

"So you're admitting you took the plant and were stupid enough to put it on an auction site right way?"

"I didn't know what else to do with it. If I killed it, it'd be worthless."

"Then how about this? Tell us about this." Jansen reached into his pocket, throwing a bagged item onto the table. "Where'd you get this?"

McCallister leaned in, trying desperately to determine what he had. She could tell that it was gold … square … a box of some sort.

Endicott bowed his head. "It was on the old man's bar that morning," he admitted. "Looked expensive."

As Jessop read him his rights, McCallister knocked lightly on the observation mirror. Promptly, Jansen entered the room.

"What the hell is that, Jansen?"

He smiled. "It's a cigarette case with engraving on the front." He grabbed a slip of paper from his pocket and handed it to her. "Dominic, *il mio grande uomo.* Alex," it read.

McCallister shook her head, not quiet fathoming the impact. "Alex, as in Alexandra … Sinclair … you mean?"

"I'd sure bet on it," he said. "Her second husband's name was Dominic Vitale, the same guy who spent the night at her apartment the day after she murdered Faraday."

She frantically scanned her mind. Then she remembered seeing the surveillance report yesterday. *Yesterday?* Yesterday seemed so very long ago. She had been rushed, trying to leave on time. She hadn't given the report a second thought, and she wasn't quite sure the first one had even amounted to much.

"You didn't miss anything, if that's what you're thinking," he reassured, sensing what she was doing. "I saw the report, too. It didn't mean anything until I saw the cigarette case on Endicott's table."

"How did you know he was her husband? I didn't."

"Jessop and I threw every background detail we could into that file after you left. Just to make sure *none* of us missed anything. Plus, if you had seen it you would have taken it from Endicott because it had her name on it."

She still wasn't satisfied, believing even more that she had done a shoddy job. Her self-castigation was interrupted by Jansen's quiet laughter.

"What?" she said, glaring at him but feeling no anger.

"Sorry. It's just funny."

"What is funny?"

"I mean no disrespect, Detective," he assured. "But you'd ream me out for doing what you're doing right now."

"Oh, and what would that be?" She smiled slightly at him so that he'd feel comfortable enough to tell her.

"It's a puzzle. There are pieces all over. Some are missing. Some don't even belong. You can imagine the big picture, but you can't see it yet. First, you find the all pieces. Then you look at every single piece from every single angle, until you can figure which fit and where. It takes time."

She smiled. She had drilled that into his impatient rookie head, enough times, apparently, that he could spout it back to her without a hint of mockery. "Did I decide the big picture, Jansen, and then go looking for the pieces?" she asked, looking him directly in the eyes. "I need to know."

"I certainly don't think you did. We all saw what you saw. I still see it. We all still see it," he said. "We had more than enough pieces to see it. Now we're just filling in the borders."

He was spot on. An arrest didn't make the remainder of the work vanish. This wasn't an hour episode on television, after all. To be thorough, everything was checked and rechecked. Every new lead was followed. All this, so Sharon Pierce could confidently tell a jury, "This is what happened. This is how it happened. This is why it happened. And sitting before you is the person who made it happen." Was that person Alexandra Sinclair? Everything said it was, and every new detail simply filled in the borders.

"You're right, Jansen," she said. When he smiled, she added, "If *you* were doing that, I would ream you out." She looked to the piece of paper again that held the engraved message. "Do you know what this Spanish or Italian is? I know 'grande' from too many espresso bars."

He informed her that he had written it down so that he could look it up. Hastily, he headed to a computer. Barely two minutes later, he said, "It's Italian. It means, 'my big man.'"

After they exchanged expressions of disgust with each other, they made a plan.

Jansen had pulled prints off the case at the Endicott house and had the lab comparing them to a set that Dominic Vitale had supplied five years ago when he was arrested for DUI. They had Alexandra's prints and would soon have the Endicotts'. If they harassed the lab enough times, they would have the results soon. Then, they'd have Vitale brought in under the guise of merely identifying stolen property. Even if it proved to be a red herring, she at least had a hunch about what Alexandra had returned to the scene to retrieve: not her own forgotten possessions, but the cigarette case belonging to her ex-husband.

McCallister took to her desk and pored over the file again, filling her mind with every detail, no matter how insignificant it seemed.

Eventually the lab called, saying that there was a partial print on the case that matched Vitale. The other prints all matched Endicott. A squad was dispatched to Vitale's residence with an officer reporting back that neither Vitale nor his car was located. McCallister put out an Attempt to Locate order and then instructed Property and Evidence on how to ensure the safety of the orchid until ownership could be established. Then she, Jansen, and Jessop called it a day.

# Chapter 12

McCallister entered the front door of her home, noticing immediately that their luggage had completed a successful journey to and from Boston. She saw Holly in the kitchen, but when she greeted her, Holly did not turn around to acknowledge her. She removed her jacket and tossed it on the big suitcase.

"Hol, I'm home," she tried again.

This time Holly turned. She was crying.

McCallister rushed to her and wrapped her arms around her, gently pulling her close. "What's wrong, honey? What happened?"

She cried even harder. "I thought it would be sweet to make you Maine lobster for dinner. But now, I can't throw Paul and Art into the pot of boiling water!"

McCallister started rocking her to mask the fact that her body shook with laughter. She glanced into the sink, and sure enough, two disoriented lobsters moved without going anywhere. "It's okay, honey," McCallister reassured her. "It was a very sweet idea. Thank you."

Holly sniffed. "You kill them, babe. You know how to be mean. Just throw their sorry asses into the pot." With both hands, she grabbed McCallister's shirt. "Just don't look into their beady little eyes, babe."

McCallister pulled away and looked into the sink again. "Why Paul and Art? You mean like Simon and Garfunkel?"

"Exactly!" Holly exclaimed. "That's what came on the radio at the grocery store while I was picking them out. It seemed fitting."

"Honey, I think it's 'One Trick Pony' not 'One Trick Lobster.'"

"Actually, it was 'Bridge Over Troubled Water.'"

With a snort from each of them, they burst out laughing. They drew each other near as their bodies convulsed, and McCallister's shirt became an inadvertent tissue.

"Just do it, Laura," she ordered. "I'll close my eyes, and you just throw them in."

McCallister looked at them yet again. She realized that they did have beady eyes. There was no curly blond hair on Art, but Paul could have passed for Paul with a little time in the sun. She laughed, realizing that personification was the quickest route to starvation or veganism. "I don't think I can do it, hon."

"Then prop the cutting board up from the sink to the pot and see if they'll go by themselves."

"How about if I just see if the store will take them back? I don't think they're suicidal. And I know for a fact that I cannot eat something with a name."

"Fine," she conceded. "I'll get the bag."

McCallister set out to grab Paul but soon determined that something was amiss. "Why did you take the bands off their claws, Hol?"

"It seemed cruel."

"Why didn't it seem cruel at the store to think about boiling them to death?"

Instantaneously, Holly started crying again. "Because I thought it would be sweet to make you Maine lobster for dinner."

Full circle. Back to the drawing board. Square one.

"It's okay, honey," McCallister reassured her as she pulled her near. "It was a very sweet idea. Thank you."

Forty-five minutes later, McCallister returned home, this time carrying a plastic container with a nameless rotisserie chicken inside. She decided not to tell Holly that the store wouldn't take Paul and Art back. She also wouldn't tell her that it took fifteen minutes in the parking lot trying to get someone to trust her enough to take them off her hands. Paul and Art had dinner plans, but she wouldn't tell her that either.

On the table, the chicken sat alongside the reheated baked potatoes and roasted vegetables that Holly had already prepared to go with the 'other' entree. All in all, it was a good salvaged meal, and they both laughed when Holly brought Boston cream pie to the table for dessert.

After dishes, they retired to the living room couch with a bottle of wine and a desperate need on McCallister's part to hold Holly as close as she could. Maybe it was the directive, "Cherish what you have, Detective," or maybe it was the same hunger she had every other day of the year. In her world, Holly indeed stood at the center.

At eight-thirty, McCallister's cell phone rang, and she cursed the cop who had the wherewithal to find Dominic Vitale and the subsequent nerve to interrupt. Holly told her not to answer it at the very second McCallister grabbed it. Seeing Kate's name, she sighed.

"This better be good, Sutter," she said without a greeting.

Kate told her she had the list of the stories T. A. Frederick had written for both publications: four appeared in *Chalkline Mysteries* and two in *Watson's Enigma*. She offered to email the list, to which McCallister responded that she did not "do email." When the lecture aimed at the technologically-challenged began, she covered the phone. "Do you want company, Hol?" she asked.

Holly agreed with the stipulation that neither of them had to move. Forcefully, McCallister interrupted Kate's lecture, ordering, "Just come over."

After having had more time to mull it over, Holly grabbed the phone and made a list of demands. "Only if you bring Claudia and another bottle of this wine. Plus, Laura and I don't have to move. Plus, you two do not talk shop! Do I make myself clear?"

With the laugh and a roll of her eyes, McCallister retrieved the phone and listened to assurances that all the demands could be met. She told her the name of the wine they were drinking and that the door would be unlocked.

McCallister and Holly resumed their coupled downtime.

A short while later, a knock at the door foretold the entry of another couple. As they entered, Kate waved a sheet of paper at McCallister and then tossed it on the table. Other than that, there existed no hint of a murder investigation. Even when McCallister and Kate snuck outside for cigarettes, there seemed to be an unspoken rule not to broach the subject.

The evening passed pleasantly.

The night passed pleasantly.

A lazy morning in bed together was interrupted only by occasional sprints to the kitchen for breakfast items and more coffee.

Even the time spent at Faraday's house that afternoon was totally void of surprises. Spangler and his students quickly finished the greenhouse inventory. There was no lone plant left standing with a clue tucked inside. There were no obscure codes to lead her to a confessionary letter. Nothing.

She said goodbye to Spangler and his students, thanking them for allowing their worlds to stop to help Faraday. They all offered to help take care of the orchids until it could be established what would happen to them. What *would* happen to them, with Faraday's sole beneficiary and only kin sitting in a jail cell? If he knew what she was going to do, why hadn't he provided for them? That, of all things, stopped her from glomming onto any sense of closure to the case.

She headed to the study to put Faraday's two letters in evidence bags, as well the issue of *Chalkline* that contained his short story. In her mind, she acknowledged Faraday's attempt to give her an out to protect herself, but it was one she didn't even need to ponder. She knew Holly would wildly paint a billboard to broadcast the love they felt for each other. She, on the other hand, was more conservative with the information. She figured that society still stereotyped every woman cop as a lesbian, so she knew it wouldn't shock the general public even if it landed on some front page in a local newspaper. She also figured her colleagues knew, because they knew her. And Greeley, he was a sucker for that Holly charm, making sure she got personally invited to picnics and Christmas parties. In addition, McCallister was not surprised by Faraday's statement that their love was palpable. She had a hard time recalling any occasion when simply looking at Holly didn't generate a soulful smile and an intense need to reach out. She laughed, thinking such an occasion was akin to telling a circus clown not to be flamboyant. She loved her deeply and knew no shame because of it.

With the evidence bags sealed and documented, she approached the tower of *Chalkline* magazines. With Kate's list in hand, she pulled the three issues that contained the work of T. A. Frederick. Sitting in the adjacent leather chair, she read and studied each one. A severed and ringed finger in the Sunday collection plate, a fisherman reeling in a floater, an amnesiac whose only memory is that of falling: all three were typical, nearly clichéd inclusions in a mystery magazine. Nothing jumped off the page. Nothing seemed to come from a tormented place of knowing. Nothing.

She took Kate's piece of paper and wrote each in code like Faraday had done with the first one. Again, none of them ended up with a position on the stagings in his greenhouse. The numbers meant nothing. Seeing it in that form and then reversing the reverse Dewey did nothing. Nothing. She scanned the tables on content, nearly expecting a "Christina Alexander" to jump off the page, what with the family's penchant for aliases. Still nothing. She scanned the magazine edges again, in quest of any paper sticking out or any gap that would indicate something was hidden within the pages. Nothing.

With a hopeful heart, she stood to face the stack of *Watson's Enigma* magazines. These, she noticed, did not sport an issue number on the spine, and she was thankful that Kate provided the complete information. She followed her finger until it came upon August 1973. She pulled it, using her other arm to provide counterweight to the shifting mountain. She tossed it to the chair and then sent her finger upward in search of March 1984.

December 1983 ... January 1984 ... February ... April ... May.

May ... April ... February ... January ... December.

She must have done the same forward and backward check a dozen times before she surrendered to the fact that it was not there. The gnawing knot in her stomach twisted, reminding her of its faithful presence. She carefully checked the date of every single magazine and then did the same to the *Chalkline* stack. Maybe he had been ashamed of the story, she thought. *Yeah, right.* She reasoned that Mr. Details would not have decade's worth of magazines with only one missing—one in which his own story happened to appear. He was stringing her along again, appealing to her sleuth.

Frustrated, she checked each stack again and then scanned every shelf in the bookcase. Again, and as expected this time, she found nothing. She retreated to the chair to read the story in the issue she did have. There, she would also find nothing, she presumed.

*Watson's Enigma* was unlike the basic mystery magazine. It was more theme-oriented and existed more as a writer's club than as merely a good read. Each month an announcement hid somewhere in the magazine, describing a challenge to authors for an upcoming issue. The themes were very eclectic, and the stories sought more to send a quake of puzzlement through the reader. Horror stories in twenty-five words or less. Murder by crowbar. Alternative history. Ghosts. Serial killers with a proclivity for the color blue.

It was easier for McCallister to see Faraday more enthralled by *Chalkline* than *Watson's*. Perhaps that was her own bias, preferring sleuth to shock. In a way, her theory made sense, though: He had been published four times in traditional and only twice in alternative.

The August 1973 issue boasted its theme on the cover: *Decapitation by Elevator.* The table of contents sent her to page forty-one for Faraday's story, "Top Dog." In it, a fellow named Jack schemed and swindled to get to the top, only to have his head arrive before him. Drollery and the macabre: only a skilled writer could meld the two without diminishing either. Certain that the Faraday house did not have an elevator out of which a severed head would roll, she dismissed the story, and her fervor to find the missing magazine intensified.

She punched in Kate's number on her cell. "Where are you?" she asked with a bit of laughter in her voice.

"Still waiting for your epiphany," Kate replied.

"In the alley?"

"No. Out front."

"Sutter, if you're going to stalk someone, it shouldn't be a cop."

"I'm not stalking you! I'm waiting for you to figure out whatever is driving you mad." She paused and then sheepishly asked, "Do you really want me to leave?"

"No!" McCallister shouted. "Stalker or not, I need your help. Light one. I'll be right there."

Mere moments later, McCallister swiped a cigarette and a cup of coffee from outstretched hands.

"See, I'm not a stalker. I'm more like your person in the corner of the ring," Kate joked. "I dope you up with nicotine and caffeine between rounds. You should thank me, not harass me. I'm doing a public service."

McCallister rolled her eyes at her and explained that she needed to get hold of a March 1984 issue of *Watson's Enigma*. "Get that little gadget of yours and tell me how to get one from the collector you found. I needed it last week."

Kate rolled her eyes right back at McCallister and informed her that the dealer lived in New Jersey. When McCallister asked whether she could find someone closer, Kate grabbed her PDA and started hunting. The two of them sat beside the car with McCallister watching the little screen, amazed.

"Can I do that on my cell?" she asked.

After Kate took a look at her phone, she said, "You have the *equivalent* of rotary dial. But it'll work for what we need." She pointed to a listing on her screen and instructed, "Start dialing."

Over the next twenty minutes, the two called every used book dealer and collector within a hundred-mile radius. Not one had a copy. Kate suggested ordering one from the dealer in New Jersey and opting for overnight shipping. "At least you'll have it by Tuesday."

McCallister looked at the huge Faraday house. She steadfastly told herself that she would not ravage the entire thing for a magazine that probably provided no clue. She would wait until Tuesday. Kate did her magic on the PDA and soon told her that the order was complete.

McCallister told her to go home, that she was going to lock up the Faraday house and do the same. As she did so, she phoned the station to inquire about any possible progress in tracking down Dominic Vitale. Every move she made that day resulted in nothing.

When she arrived home, Holly was nowhere to be found until she peeked out the back window. Holly's studio was a separate building set back on the property. There, she painted, taught classes, and took care of the business side of her art. McCallister could see her standing at an easel, her hand moving on the canvas, stopping occasionally for a dab from the palette she held in her other hand. McCallister found it an overwhelmingly sensual experience to watch her paint: her intent, her touch, her gentleness, the way she bit her tongue when concentrating on finer details. For this reason, there were self-imposed rules about entering the studio, and as she continued to watch her, she knew today was not a day to be testing them. Instead, she went out on the patio, took a seat, and simply observed from a safe distance.

Eventually, Holly turned and saw her sitting there, her face widening in smile, her paintbrush waving a greeting. A pantomimed discussion resulted in McCallister convincing Holly to continue her work. The occasional looks she received from Holly contented her, and she let her mind drift, pondering what stopped the gnawing knot inside her from unwinding.

Again, the evening passed pleasantly.

The night passed pleasantly.

Monday morning, however, told a different story.

She hadn't even stepped foot out of her vehicle in the station's lot before the press bombarded her.

"What's your reaction to Alexandra Sinclair getting bail, Detective?" one reporter yelled, and every other question pelting her resonated with the same perplexity. "Should somebody who could kill her own brother be allowed to walk our streets?"

Although McCallister found herself utterly shocked by the news, she stoically replied, "I trust the system." She smiled at them, adding, "Let's let it work, shall we?"

She spied Kate in the crowd and received a look that seemed to assure McCallister that giving her a heads-up had been impossible. She entered the station and headed directly to Greeley's office, with Jansen and Jessop falling in line to follow her.

Greeley looked up at her. "I take it you heard," he said.

"Not before the press."

"It just happened. I just got off the phone with Sharon," he explained. "She's none too happy, either. Said the judge figured that since she was alone in the world now, she couldn't be a threat to anyone."

"It's not always about threat," McCallister said snidely. "Sometimes it's just a matter of what's right."

"What's right, Laura, is that we get this wrapped up and airtight and then move on. Did you figure out how he knows procedure?"

"He's a mystery buff."

"Did you figure out why he messed with us?"

McCallister thought for a moment, and then she said, "He knew what she was going to do, but he didn't have it in him, I guess, to stop her, even though he said he was going to try. He 'messed with us' to make sure we got what we needed for the case ... and for her to get help."

"It's not our job to get her help. It's our job to get the facts and let the courts decide how justice is best served."

"I don't think he expected us to help her, Cap," she reasoned. "I think he was just making sure we *got* the facts."

Then why were they cryptic? Why didn't he just put it all out there? Why the games? His last hurrah? His one and only chance to pit his sleuth against hers? And why let his orchids die with him? The knot in her stomach had many strangling threads.

Greeley interrupted the questions McCallister would not ask aloud, saying, "Well, if the guy sat by knowing what she was going to do— putting his head on her chopping block—it sounds like he needed as much help as he thought she needed." He shook his head. "That's damned sick. So get all your stuff together, get it to Sharon, and get moving. I have a hundred other things for you to do. Or take your vacation. Maybe you need one more than I thought. Whatever—just get moving."

She nodded respectfully and retreated. As she headed for her desk, she turned to look at Jansen and Jessop, wondering what they were thinking. Surprisingly, they both smiled at her and nodded simultaneously.

"We'll keep an eye on her," Jessop whispered before scooting away so it didn't look as though they were conspiring.

Jansen did the same. "Like you say, guts don't go by the book."

McCallister did as she was told. By eleven, she completed a delivery to Sharon's office. She handed over what she had, including the information she gleaned over the weekend from Faraday's letters, Endicott's thefts, and even the short story. It all bolstered the conclusion, and yet, McCallister had that feeling she often found when reading mysteries. It was all there—mystery solved—and yet a third of the book remained.

"Find Vitale," the DA ordered. "A witness or an accessory will seal the deal."

McCallister returned to the station, keeping quiet and avoiding people as best she could. Her mind returned to the case she had been working on before Faraday's had taken over. It was a burglary that had taken place in an electronics store while surveillance cameras rolled; no sleuth required.

# Chapter 13

Tuesday arrived with McCallister's hopes on the rise.

She met Dr. Spangler at the Faraday house so he could take care of the orchids. As he did so, she watched the yellow police tape flap in the chilly April air. As long as she kept the scene active—and under Greeley's radar—Alexandra could not enter, could not take over, could not destroy what Faraday loved.

Then, she drove to Timmer's to grab a cup of coffee, checked in at the station, switched cars, and drove aimlessly. She set the volume on the car's police radio so low that it was nearly inaudible. Her cell phone sat idly on the passenger seat, and her hands nearly twitched, waiting for the moment it would announce that Kate had received the copy of *Watson's Enigma*.

Eventually, that moment arrived. She was sitting in the parking lot of the burglarized electronics store, completing a report. As the phone sounded and vibrated on the seat, she reminded herself that the story would probably dead-end like the others, and yet, she hoped. It made the gnawing knot tighten, like a homing device going off, telling her a target neared.

After taking a deep breath, she answered.

Kate announced, "I've got the magazine. Do you want me to drop it off?"

McCallister asked where she was, and the two made a plan to meet in front of Faraday's house.

Ten minutes later, she leaned against her car, ripped open the envelope, and withdrew her prize. The front of the worn magazine sported: *Ten Terrifying Tales: How to Fake Your Own Murder.*

Her jaw dropped. Like an old, rusted cog, her mind seized. She wanted to laugh. She wanted to scream angry things at Faraday. She wanted to vomit from the split-second thought flashing through her mind: *Alexandra Sinclair is innocent.* Inside and out, paradoxical reactions surfaced and sunk. She felt too many things all at once. She wanted too many things simultaneously. But more than anything, she hungered to know.

Nearly shaking from an influx of adrenalin, her hands fumbled to the table of contents and then to the story's first page. She greedily consumed.

### Rat-A-Tat Tattoo

"You piece of human crap!" Shorty Malone bellowed with a sneer. "You couldn't pull the trigger if your life depended on it."

"I'll do it, Shorty. If you don't back off, I'll do it."

"You slept with my girl! Why should I back off?"

A small leery crowd gathered at the end of the block. A man in a white apron quickly stuck his head out a storefront and then retreated with just as much haste. One brave or reckless man stood to watch. A woman ran, dragging her dog by its leash. Several people ducked into doorways.

"*Your* girl?" Hank yelled. "Your *girl* seems to think you're a nut case."

"Nuts? Well, at least, I've got a pair of them. You don't!" Shorty taunted and then laughed. "I bet you couldn't pull the trigger with her either." He bent over in the throes of laughter.

Hank aimed the gun at him. Gasps erupted from the quickly dispersing crowd.

Shorty stood straight, jutting out his chest and stiffening his spine. "Do it!" he screamed as his ears detected sirens in the distance. "Do it, you piece of crap!"

In the last blink of an eye, Shorty rushed him, and just before he reached him, he stopped and raised his hands high like a preacher on a Sunday pulpit.

A deafening shot rang out.

Shorty fell to the ground and didn't move. In fact, he never moved again. A dazed Hank merely stared down at him, the gun now hanging limp in his hand.

Within minutes, two police officers arrived at the scene. Their guns were drawn and pointed at Hank. "Just drop it, son," one of them ordered.

But Hank didn't move, but for a much different reason than why Shorty didn't move. Shock seized him and would not let go.

An officer inched closer to him and stealthily confiscated the gun without resistance. He removed handcuffs from his belt and hurried to restrain Hank before his ability to think returned.

The other officer knelt next to Shorty and felt his neck and then his wrist for a pulse. He raised an eyelid to check his pupils. He saw the big, dark red blotch widen on the left side of Shorty's flannel-shirted chest. "Straight through the heart, I'd say. He's dead," he shouted to the other officer. "I'll call the wagon."

Hank sat motionlessly in the back of the squad car as the officers hastily took statements from a few gawkers in the vicinity. Soon, an ambulance arrived and prepared Shorty for transport to the backlogged city morgue.

A short time later, the officers slid into the front seat of the squad. One of them glanced into the rearview mirror, stared at Hank's ashen face, and shook his head. "Just because somebody tosses you his gun and dares you to shoot him, doesn't give you the right to do it, son."

\* \* \* \* \*

Three days passed before the overworked Dr. Mathers even had the chance to begin work on Case Number 166953-0114. He quickly matched that trivial number to the correct toe tag and wheeled the gurney down the hall and into his work area. Pulling back the sheet, his eyes ran the length of Todd "Shorty" Malone, whose skin color matched the gray striping in his flannel shirt. It used to be that cadavers got to Mathers in naked form, but the backlog took its toll on attendants as well, rendering used-to-be's a luxury. Nowadays he disrobed bodies right on the table and collected personal effects as he went along.

He grabbed the shoes from the gurney and threw them into a box. Then he snatched the file, took a cursory glance, and looked to his watch. The attached note, "GSW Homicide w/ Witnesses," ensured that his job would be quick. Find the bullet, its trajectory, the distance from gun to wound, and bam! He could eat lunch when the rest of the world ate lunch. That, too, was a luxury nowadays.

Old Mathers had long, long ago hardened to the sight of a dead body. He had to; it was essential to his job unless, of course, he wanted to flip burgers at the dive down the street. To him, bodies were not people anymore. They were hunks of meat that he sliced and diced, sewed back up, and then signed over to a mortuary for them to instill the dignity that he could not see in their putrefying states. The day they became anything other than that was the day he'd willfully glom onto the dive's spatula and ask, "How would you like that cooked, lady? Medium well? Excellent choice."

He grabbed his scissors and began cutting the pant legs with a jaggy upward motion. He did the same to a pair of blue and gray striped boxer shorts. If he had the time, he probably would have unbuttoned the shirt, but instead he used the same upward motion. He set the scissors down with a clank on the metal table and then grabbed the sides of the cut flannel to give him direct access to the bullet wound. "A perfect shot to the heart," he recalled reading in the file. Simple.

But in one swift motion, old Mathers' mechanical and cold life changed.

111

He froze in mid-pull when the torso came into view. Little black diagonal lines seemed to stack up on each other, from shoulders to navel, marking the precise location for the Y incision he would make to flay the body from stem to stern. Black words read, "cut doc sew what?"

Mathers cussed, figuring some sick attendant had played a dirty trick. He swabbed a cotton tip with alcohol and then rubbed roughly on one of the lines, expecting it to dissolve, fade, disappear. But it didn't. Tattoos proved far more permanent than permanent marker.

In disbelief, with bile rising in his throat, he looked to the cadaver— the last one that would ever be a hunk of meat.

There was an X in the upper right part of the abdomen, with the words, "poke a probe," telling Mathers where to insert his device if he needed a core temperature.

Where the shirt collar would have covered the neck, there was another X and the words, "jab a jugular tube," telling the mortician where to insert his needle.

On the side of his abdomen, yet another X sat beside the words, "tap a trocar," telling the mortician where to insert another needle for cavity embalming.

When he ran out of sickening words on the man—on this, the body of Todd "Shorty" Malone—he turned him over, nearly dropping him on the floor. Down the spine on both smooth sides, more tattoos ran—these, never having had a chance to heal, telling Mathers...

*Tell Hank a blank is a prank.*
*Cost me 10 x 40 for this rigamorty. —Shorty.*

Stupefied, she waited for her brain to start firing again. When she felt it finally do so, she swallowed hard, plastered a smile on her face, and turned to Kate. "Thanks for helping me get this," she said to her. She pulled money out of her pocket and handed it over to cover the expense. "You're a good friend."

Kate twisted her face to form a quizzical expression. "Did it help?" she asked. "Did you get anything?"

"Just more questions," she replied. "But I expected as much." She smiled at her again. "You might have better luck following your colleagues around today instead of me." Then, she stared at her, hoping she got the hint to leave without her having to say it.

"They're camped out at Sinclair's place, hoping she'll talk to them."

"That would make for a good story."

Kate twisted her face again. "You want me to leave, huh?" When McCallister nodded, she amicably said, "You've got it. Just let me know if you need me in the corner of the ring … or if there are crumbs to be had." She smiled, got in her car, and left.

McCallister headed to her own car, sliding into the driver's seat and promptly lighting a cigarette. The knot in her stomach tightened and loosened, allowing anger, guilt, confusion, and shock to weave themselves into her being. But, they were distractions; she needed her thoughts to disjoin from her feelings. Intuition had its place, but emotions did not belong in an investigation. She took a long drag from her cigarette and tilted her head back onto the headrest.

Was it possible that Faraday had committed suicide and framed his sister? *Yes*, she readily acknowledged. She reasoned that was why he had removed the copy of *Watson's Enigma,* so Shorty Malone wouldn't put the idea in her head. He wanted her focused on murder. He wanted her to keep gathering the 'facts' that would keep his sister locked up. But, that still didn't account for his changing the will ... unless the sole purpose was to give her a motive for murder. But, he changed it at her insistence; Alexandra admitted that. Then he had simply manipulated her, knowing her greed. And he had manipulated the detective he claimed to respect. She admitted that there couldn't have been too much respect if he figured he could dupe her that easily. The anger roiled within her, and she tried desperately to stay in her head.

She grabbed her cell and called Hastings.

"I heard you never made it to Maine," he said. "Now you owe me double." He expected ribbing in return.

"I'll pay, Hastings. Just name it," she replied with total seriousness. "But at the moment, I need your help." She paused and then said, "I'm getting my reports done, so I need to double-check a couple of things with you."

He was taken aback by the lack of banter. "What do you need, Laura?"

"Did Faraday have any tattoos?" She knew it was a long shot, but she also knew she was not about to ignore any possibility. When Hastings said that he didn't, she asked, "Can you tell me what your case number is for him?" She could hear him rifling through files on his desk. When he read the number to her, she stared at Shorty Malone's case number in the magazine. She knew the odds of them matching were even more remote than Faraday sporting telltale tattoos.

She thanked Hastings and quickly ended the call. Hurriedly, she wrote the fictional autopsy number on a piece of paper and stared at it, wondering if it meant something, just as the cigar box in the other story had. When no answer came to her, she shoved the paper into her pocket.

Then, she dialed Sharon Pierce's office and asked her secretary for the date of Alexandra's preliminary hearing. The woman told her it was Friday at eleven. McCallister reasoned that as long as Alexandra was out on bail and had not been bound over for trial, the situation was both livable and salvageable. In her mind, she vowed to make things right before Alexandra stepped foot into that courtroom, either by proving that Faraday had killed himself or by doing whatever she had to do to make the knot in her stomach disentangle.

She quickly finished the report on the burglary and then headed back to the station. She tossed the report into Greeley's in-box and then headed back to Faraday's in her own car, parking a block away. She texted a message to Holly, "I will probably be late. I love you," and then she walked to the front door.

In her mind, she chose to believe that Faraday was still stringing her along, that somewhere in that big house the missing magazine sat with a letter enfolding the pages of his story. She had not readily known how to get a hold of a back issue, and since both of them still resided in a world of rotary phones or the like, she surmised that he wouldn't have either. In other words, he hadn't expected her to find one … or at least not this soon. He was waiting for his moment to reveal it, but she was determined to find it first. He banked that sleuth would prevail over ransack, but he had miscalculated. She readied herself to ransack.

She stood in the foyer and waited until Holly's text reply arrived. "I love you, too. See you soon," it read. She smiled fondly at that hope and turned off her cell phone.

She moved into the sitting room, all its painting staring at her as if they somehow knew what was coming. She removed each from its place on the wall. She shook them. She checked each for something embedded in the picture itself, a clue or a code like the one in Holly's—anything. She felt each back for the bulge of a secret. Finding nothing, she pulled the safe open, looking for a false bottom or side, like the cigar box. She knocked on every piece of paneling on the wall. She examined couch cushions and the chaise lounge. She rolled up the Oriental rug for a glimpse. She looked over, under, up, down, and sideways.

She did the same in the dining room. She did the same in the pantry and the kitchen … the laundry room … the sitting porch … the bathroom … the study … the living room. She returned to his command center and spied every note he had penned. Where was the one that said, "Hide the copy of *Watson's Enigma* in the _____"?

"Where did you hide it, Faraday?" she shouted into the silence. "You wouldn't have gotten rid of it. I know you."

Determinedly, she climbed the steps to the second floor. In the hall, she again checked every painting and wall. She entered a large bedroom that had its own bathroom, dressing room, and sleeping porch. As she spied the items on the dressers and in the drawers, it became clear that she was in Faraday's parents' room. She surmised that it was exactly as they had left it when the last one died. "See, Faraday," she shouted. "You can't let go. Where is the goddamn magazine and the letter you owe me?"

When her search of the room was complete, she entered the main bathroom, finding it completely devoid of personal items. The next room appeared to be a guest bedroom, and again, it contained nothing personal; it merely existed as unused space in a single man's large home.

Then she entered what she was sure was Alexandra's old room. It boasted lavender paint and stylish curtains. She immediately walked to the window, wondering if boys had really climbed up on summer mornings. The idea of a parade of them disgusted her, too, but she imagined that it was minuscule compared to what a tormented brother might have felt.

She searched. Knowing that Alexandra had made a life of her own, it did not surprise her to find very few personal items in there either. A hairbrush, a robe, slippers, a box with two syringes and a long-ago expired bottle of insulin, and a few old 45s were all that remained. Everything else was impalpable memory.

As she turned to leave, Faraday's story ran through her mind again and a sadness swept over her. What had happened in this house? What had happened to Alexandra? *Was* she born abusive and vindictive? Her hate and anger—the venom she herself had witnessed—did not dissipate by simply entertaining the notion that Faraday had killed himself. Even proving that he did take his own life and framed her in the process, did not leave her innocent. There were enough secrets and sins to go around. She thought of the boy Albert, letting his stress float away as he smoked a cigarette behind the shed.

"The shed!" she yelled, feeling the timely arrival of an epiphany. The cigar box rendered a clue. Why not the shed?

With great strides, she raced back through the elder Faradays' bedroom and onto the sitting porch. A smug smile made itself at home on her face as her eyes scanned the back lot. Only there wasn't a shed. No matter how many times her eyes made the circuit, she found no shed. Her smugness turned to diffidence as she left to continue her search.

The last room upstairs, she easily deduced, belonged to Faraday. She entered, and suddenly, she felt like an intruder in his home. His room, for sure, was exactly as he left it the day he died. Other than a sweep by Bartholomew, Faraday had been the last one in there. She wondered if he woke that morning knowing he would not be returning. If he did, that didn't seem like sufficient motivation to rise and shine.

She respectfully went through his things. Again, there seemed to be little that was personal. The items were functional in nature: clothes, a hairbrush, a nail clipper. Things he needed, but nothing that said anything about him. Even the drapery and bed linen were dispassionate: beiges and muted blues. Under the bed, however, she found a long storage box chock-full of baseball cards. Most were organized in Faraday's fastidious way, but nearly a third of the box simply held unopened packages. She surmised that he either reached an age where they didn't matter anymore or that something had taken the joy out of it for him. So while the box was the only truly personal thing in the room, it still seemed half-spoken.

By the time McCallister headed for staircase, the sun was setting, leaving the house in ominous shadows. She sat on the top step and tried to determine her next move. What had she missed? She knew it was there. It had to be there.

Suddenly, she heard the front door open, and instinctively, her hand reached inside her jacket to her gun.

"Laura! ... Laura, I know you're here."

It was Greeley. So much for staying under the radar.

"Laura!" he yelled again.

"I'm here, Cap," she contritely replied, waiting for the wrath that bore her name.

"Well, get over here where I can see you."

Slowly, she rose on the creaky step and made her descent. Wincing inside, she stood before him and waited.

"So did you find what you're looking for?" he asked.

She was perplexed by the absence of anger in his voice and did not answer.

"Do you really think I'm that stupid, Laura? I know something's not sitting right with you. I also know that you've never let me down."

Still she remained silent. Still she struggled to fathom. If he knew, there was no way she had not infuriated him.

"I do trust you, Laura. But, I will *not* tolerate sneaking around behind my back. You get away with enough as it is. But, this—this crosses all lines!"

There it was.

"You need to do something, I want to know about it," he said.

"You told me to wrap it up and get moving."

"What was I supposed to say? Let everything else slide and take your time? Boy, that would make me a good captain, huh? But, this crap of disappearing, turning your phone off—that won't cut it with me. And sitting alone in the dark at a crime scene— I don't want *any* of you doing that. It's not how we work. We watch each others' backs."

116

"You're right." She wasn't about to argue with him.

"So, five minutes later: Did you find what you're looking for?"

"No."

"Do you know what you're looking for?"

"Yes. ... No. ... I think so."

"Boy, this one's got you!" He shook his head. "Where's the cocky detective we all know and fear—I mean, respect?" He nearly laughed and then grew serious. "What is it, Laura? What's got you?"

"It was too easy, too neat."

"They happen that way sometimes."

"All along my gut has said something's missing."

"You don't think Sinclair did it?"

"I'm totally convinced that she did it and then totally unconvinced all over again."

"Well, if the same thing happens to a jury, it's reasonable doubt, and we're screwed. So that, above all else, is what you need to trust. So yes, you're right to keep looking, but would you *please* follow my rules? They can't be that hard for you."

She nodded. It felt better to know she didn't have to slink around in the shadows.

"Now, turn your phone on," he ordered, and then he waited until she did so. "Are you ready to get out of here, or do you want me to radio in for someone?"

"I'm going. I'm going. I'll come back in the morning."

She locked up and then started for her car. As she walked, she called Holly, hoping she hadn't needed to get in touch with her. They made a plan to grab a bite to eat and then go to the gym so McCallister could work out. Her head ached from exhaustion, but her body screamed with a need to move.

# Chapter 14

McCallister returned to the Faraday house Wednesday morning to be greeted by Jansen and Jessop at the front door.

"Cap?" she asked, figuring they had been summoned by the powers that be. When they both nodded, the three of them laughed.

"That's good," she reasoned. "The more eyeballs on this big house the better."

She directed them to the study and showed them a copy of *Watson's Enigma*. "There's one of these hiding in this house. I'm sure of it. I searched the entire house and didn't find it. I need you guys to check me. Go through this house, and do it with the assumption that I am a total moron. I know that's hard for you to assume but try it anyway." She laughed, and it was a welcome change. "Whoever finds March 1984, I'll buy you lunch." She paused and then added, "Whoever doesn't find it ... has to reimburse me for the lunch I just bought your partner. Now, go, you two. Show me up! Make me look like a complete idiot."

They eagerly took on the task. As they left the room, she informed them, "I'm going out to check the grounds and then the guesthouse."

She exited through the front door and began walking the parameter of the house. Her cell phone rang in her pocket, and she half-expected it to be Greeley making sure she was following his rules. Instead, it was Hastings.

"I've got an Authorization to Transfer Possession on Faraday with a request to permit immediate cremation," he said. "Any objections?"

"Who the hell requested it?"

"The sister by way of the family lawyer."

"That's bullshit! The so-called family lawyer is representing her!" she spat. "Since when do we release a body to the goddamn person charged with the murder?"

"The law doesn't say otherwise. Legally, she is next-of-kin. Actually, she's his only kin. She's not doing anything wrong if my work is done. *Is* my work done, Laura?"

McCallister scrambled to think of something. She did not want to voice the possibility that it wasn't murder; there was nothing to back it up other than a decades-old story Faraday had penned. Adding that to the mix was premature. "Find a way to stall it." She grabbed at straws of ridiculousness. "Did you count every hair on the man's head like I asked, Hastings? Sometimes a whole case can turn on a strand of hair."

Cautiously, he laughed. "Not usually when it's still attached to the victim's own head. But I hear you. I'll find a way to hold off, and I'll see if there's a way Sharon can stop it."

"Thank you," she said. "And here's the moment where you tell me I owe you again. Go ahead."

"This one's on the house."

She repeated the phrase "on the house" as she put the phone back in her pocket. "How about *in* the house?" she asked. "Faraday, you told me you'd give me everything I needed for the investigation. Where the hell is it? If you honestly loved your sister, you won't let her rot if she didn't do it."

Eventually, she stood in the backyard, and once again, she scanned the area as though a nonexistent shed would magically appear. Shaking her head, she began looking for an entrance to a storm shelter or a root cellar. This was the Midwest, and if an old house didn't have a basement, it usually had one or the other. When she located a cellar, she entered with flashlight drawn. Finding nothing but dampness and cobwebs, she retreated and looked up at the house. She called Jessop and told him to look for an attic.

As she headed toward the guesthouse, she found herself glancing expectantly into the alley. At that moment, she would have welcomed Kate in the corner of the ring, propping her up between rounds. She surely felt beaten, and yet, something animalistic drove her to want the bell to ring again so she could come out swinging. The need to throw a knockout blow propelled her.

She checked the guesthouse again, just as she had done several times before. She remembered that looking at Mr. Probable Cause raised the possibility that Faraday had killed himself. The whole point of his intricate charade was to get her to find the code that led her to the letter and story in the *Chalkline*. So there had to be something pointing her to the next. Something she couldn't see. Something that frustrated her beyond the point of reason.

Defeated, she sat on the floor next to the bed and began pulling the journals out from under it. When they came out upside down, "TAF" looked like "FAT." She recalled refusing to read every thought Faraday had ever penned. That fat chance was quickly turning into her last chance. She pulled out the stacks, and expecting no less from Faraday, she found them ordered chronologically. There were fifty-three of them … five per stack, plus one stack of three. Each journal housed about six-months worth of entries. Fifty divided by two … plus eighteen months … twenty-six and a half years! Coaxed by the absurdity of it all, she realized that she would have been eight years old, probably not yet knowing how to write in cursive, when he started the first one.

Despite wanting to begin at the end and work backwards, she began in the order they were presented, trusting his logical mind. She found entries regarding the initial construction of his greenhouse, new orchid acquisitions, memories. Occasionally, she'd run across a card from his command center with a code on the front and a date on the back. The date corresponded to the journal entry, and she quickly figured out that these were plants he had lost. He was holding true to what the orchid magazine's article said: *careful, handwritten accounts of life and death.* She paid attention to each section of code that pertained to position, both hoping and dreading that one would be a clue by indicating a staging that did not exist in his greenhouse.

Soon, she looked up to see Jansen and Jessop standing in the doorway. By the looks on their faces, she knew they bore no good news. "Thanks for trying, guys." She told them to head out for lunch, that she was going to continue going through the journals and that she would catch up with them later.

She resumed her study, not caring that it snowed on Christmas morning in 1983 or that New Year's Day, 1984, broke clear. She skimmed the following days and weeks, looking for a mention of the *Watson's Enigma* story he had published then. She assumed that he simply didn't put mention of T. A. Frederick into his personal writing. That made sense to her when she considered his shame in having to admit to alter ego's existence.

Half an hour later, she answered her ringing cell phone. Jansen's eager voice said, "Sinclair's on the move. She's doubled-parked in front of a flower shop."

McCallister laughed at herself when she wondered whether double-parking was severe enough to peg her for violating conditions of her bail. She instructed, "Follow her, Jansen, and let me know."

She returned to the journals, flipping through each one looking for codes. When she closed out the latter half of 1984, she put it into its rightful place in the stack and grabbed the next. She sat for a moment and stretched, suddenly feeling the need for a cigarette and the bathtub-size cup of coffee that Jessop had found for her. She dismissed the notion

121

and continued her task.

Ten minutes later her phone rang again. This time Kate's enthusiastic voice declared, "Sinclair did do it! She's in a church on the east side of town. Is that a sign of guilt or what?"

McCallister knew it wasn't to make funeral arrangements. She wanted to incinerate her brother just like she wanted to do to his orchids. She repeated the same directive to Kate, "Follow her, and let me know."

With Sinclair in motion and three people in pursuit, she herself needed to move ... and seek out a cigarette. As she rose, however, the craving left her instantaneously when she realized that something was inside the baseboard heat register halfway behind the bed. She flew to it and peered in. A plastic zipper bag held the missing copy of *Watson's Enigma!* She pulled. She twisted. She kicked. Then, like a bullet from her gun, she sped to the kitchen in search of a screwdriver or a knife. Quickly, she returned with a utility knife. Her hands shook as she worked to unscrew the cover. She had one screw removed when her cell went off.

"What now?" she snapped.

"She's at the Unitarian Church on Elm," Jansen said with a cautious voice.

"I know where she is!" she shouted at him. "I found the magazine! I found it, Jansen."

"Good job, Detective," he acknowledged and then asked, "Do you still want me to follow her?" When he received a brusque go-ahead, he disconnected.

She worked to remove another screw. When she pulled it free, she focused on the next, while giving the cover a pull to see whether the last two mattered. She got the third one free to the sound of her cell phone.

She spat, "What the hell is with you guys?"

"Don't yell at me!" Kate spat right back. "You told me to follow her!"

As she tugged on the cover, she half-heartedly apologized.

Just as the cover dislodged, Kate said, "She's leaving the church."

"Okay. Whatever. Thanks," she replied dismissively as she put the cover aside and prepared to retrieve her next reward.

The interior of the heating duct was covered with a thick layer of dust, but the plastic bag was spotless and neatly folded to the size of the magazine inside. She seized it and sat back against the wall. With utter triumph, she spied a sheet of paper sticking out of the book. She took a deep breath and removed the magazine from the bag.

She carefully withdrew the paper, unconcerned with the pages it marked; she already knew. She looked to the familiar handwriting and began to read.

*Detective McCallister,*

*First of all, I commend your stamina. You have hung in there with me, and you are about to see the end for which you have worked so hard.*

"You have no f-ing idea, Faraday! But I got you, didn't I?"

*I am trusting that this is Wednesday. I have been without breath and the things I love for a week now. That is hard for me to imagine in this moment, where my hand can still move the pen across this page. I hope there is peace. I crave peace.*

Things had been so hectic that she had to stop and think if his plan had unfolded properly. She acknowledged that it was indeed Wednesday, and then her sense of triumph evaporated as she fathomed the gravity of what he had just said. His body deteriorated in a morgue … with his sister requesting its immediate cremation. The passage of a week was accurate, and she found herself honestly hoping that he had indeed found peace.

*I am trusting that Dorsey got help for Alexandra. I pray he did, and I pray that it was long enough for them to figure out what is wrong with her and convince her to get help. I pray with every cell of me that it succeeded.*

That was a different story, one that McCallister did not care to think about. She had no control over a defense attorney.

*For she is about to taste freedom again.*
*She did not murder me.*
*I murdered me.*

A myriad of feelings within her vied to surface first, but the jostling for position stopped any of them from getting out. The jumble halted reasoning and left her stunned. She swallowed hard to force them all back down, and then she tried to gauge the knot in her stomach. It had slackened considerably.

*I have the beginnings of Alzheimer's, Detective. My body is strong, but I am starting to lose what is important to me. I began to notice things last year, like going to water my beautiful orchids only to find them already drenched, reading a page in a book and having no idea what I just read.*

*I do not want to be here if I cannot recognize what I love the most. Would you, Detective?*

Thoughts rushed to her mind that did not belong at a crime scene. His simple question made it personal again, and her mind frantically raced to Holly. She could not help envisioning her face while trying to shutter her mind to the thought of not being able to recognize her, of not being able to be replenished by the love she faithfully found there. And then, one feeling got to the surface first and spontaneously escaped. Utter despair took over, and tears filled her eyes. From nearly the moment the whole investigation had begun, he brought Holly into it: the painting, the letter about seeing her, identifying her as who she loved the most in life. And now—now he dared asked her to question whether she wanted to be a part of the world if she couldn't recognize her! She wanted to scream from a place so deep inside that it mortified her.

She dropped the letter and shot to a standing position, reprimanding herself for weakness, for getting sucked in, for letting a dead man peer into her own eyes when it was her job to look into his. With desperate strides, she left the guesthouse and sped to the alley. She fumbled for the lighter and pack of cigarettes in her pocket. She lit up with a mighty inhalation and then looked to the sky, the budding trees, the birds, the sunshine. She sought them out for distraction, but all she saw was life—another one of those disturbing contradictions.

Urgently in need of her intellect and hard exterior, she kicked rocks as she walked from one end of the alley to the other. And then, unsure whether salvation or damnation, she watched Kate's car slowly approach.

Kate got out and stared at her, studied her with squinting eyes. Finally, she asked, "Are you just bitchy at me or is something wrong?"

McCallister didn't answer. What was she supposed to say? *Yes, Kate, as a matter of fact, something is wrong. Faraday killed himself, and I arrested his sister for it. Then, I stupidly allowed the dead man to walk around in my soul and make me terrified of losing the woman I love. Other than that, everything's just great. And how are you? Got any coffee?*

Kate stared her down. "Will you answer the damn question? If you're mad at me, I can deal with it. If something's wrong, I want to know." When McCallister didn't answer, she yelled, "If it's about the case, I'm not snooping. I just want to know that you're okay." When she still didn't answer, Kate walked to her car and got her cup of coffee. "I'll trade you. Bitch me out or tell me what's wrong, and I'll give you the coffee."

McCallister could not help smiling as Kate approached. She outstretched her hand.

"Tell me first," Kate ordered, jerking the cup back. "I know what a weasel you can be."

She smiled again. "There seems to be a chink in my armor," she admitted and then waited for Kate to hand over the coffee. She took a big swig.

"Big chink?"

"Huge chink," she answered. "So big that it feels like I'm inside out. That's not good—not here, not now." She swallowed hard, resisting tears with all her strength.

Kate nodded her head with understanding. "Chink repair?"

"Please."

With feigned skepticism, Kate looked into her eyes. "And you'll remember that you asked for it? That you even said please?"

A laugh erupted from McCallister, and she knew that restoration was already underway. She nodded submissively.

Sensing the same thing, Kate laughed with her. "So, are you bitchy at me or just a bitch?"

"A bitch," she declared.

"Big bitch?"

"Huge bitch!" she answered, feeling her exterior harden and her mind regain control. "Now get the hell out of here and quit bothering me."

Before turning to leave, Kate said, "I would be happy to." She got in her car and yelled, "Sinclair is at home again. Where should I be?"

McCallister raised the paper cup in salute. "Apparently getting yourself another cup of coffee." She smiled at her once more and returned to the guesthouse.

She grabbed the letter, and instead of huddling with it like a docile fool, she stood in the center of the room to read.

*As Thaddeus, I went to Dr. Robert Roth, and he confirmed what I suspected. He explained the stages, and I have done my best to keep my mind sharp, but I know I am losing, fast.*

*I tried carefully to broach the subject with Alex, the simple idea that*

125

I would not be here. Ironically, that is the moment I fathomed the line with her that I must never cross. As much as she has hated me, she always depended on me to be there. A paradox, isn't it? The idea of my not being here produced a rage in her that was unlike anything I had ever seen. I am banking on the fact that her rage was there when someone—probably you—told her that I was dead. A shock, a catalyst: something to get people to see in her what she is so good at keeping secret from strangers. Something to draw attention to the fact that she needs help. Something for Dorsey to use.

A sick game I have played? Yes, and I truly hope that you forgive me for using you, for burdening you with this. Please understand that I ran out of choices. Alex still has life ahead of her. I want her to know peace as well.

What you need to know...

I changed my will and increased my life insurance to give her an obvious motive. I invited her for dinner ... on a Wednesday so poor Jenny would find me the next morning when she came to clean. I faked my last journal entry. I mixed the poison and wiped the bottle clean. I manipulated Alex to get her fingerprints where I needed them. I pushed her into an argument—loud enough for Doug to hear when he sneaks out for his seven o'clock cigarette. (Audrey knows, by the way; she watches him from the window, but he doesn't need to know that.) I pushed Alex's buttons. I scratched her. I set the living room up to look like a scene from one of those mysteries we both love. How did I do, Detective?

If it is Wednesday and Alex understands, then I can rest. Please tell her I did it because I love her and not to be cruel. Please tell her I said to find a way to be happy—now that she sees what remains when all seems lost.

And you, Detective... Thank you!

Cherish what you have.

Keep your mind sharp...

126

Closed off from any feeling, she went through the list of what he had given her, making sure everything countered their conclusions and still supported the evidence they had gathered. It all added up—other than the discrepancy between "his seven o'clock cigarette" and Penning's report of having been outside at eight-thirty. That could be easily explained. Perhaps he had been delayed by the rain.

Recognizing that he had signed the letter differently, she reread the last line, "There's the cost I pay in what I write everyday. —Faraday." She smiled and caught herself before boasting aloud to Faraday that her mind was as sharp as a tack. With a dire need to keep it impersonal, she vowed not to address him ever again.

Then she flipped to the short story in *Watson's Enigma* and read from the last page, "Cost me 10 x 40 for this rigamorty. —Shorty." It was a morbid rhyme that occasionally got stuck in her head. Perhaps if she had read the letter and then the story, like she was supposed to, it wouldn't have made sense so quickly. As it stood, Shorty Malone had been a driving force since the day prior.

She reasoned, "'The cost I pay' would be 10x40 ... 'in what I write everyday.'" Again she smiled. "Dewey, Dewey, Dewey. Volume 10, bottom of the second stack, page 40, or reverse for volume 40, page 10. Not bad for the code-challenged." Her cockiness had returned. The chink was gone.

As she pulled the tenth journal, her phone sounded, and she tried to guess who had the nerve. It was Jansen. "We've got Vitale," he said, his own cockiness making its presence known. "He was on his way into Alexandra Sinclair's."

"I don't think it matters anymore, Jansen," she said. "I have a lot to fill you in on."

He completely dismissed what she said. "He said the cigarette case isn't his."

McCallister was taken aback. "How the hell can he deny it? His damn print is on it."

"Exactly what I told him. So I asked about the night of the murder," he explained. "He got all self-righteous and said he didn't have to answer any questions about that."

"Oh, did he now?" Irrelevant or not—she did not appreciate anyone lying to cops. "Did he ask for a lawyer?"

"No, apparently the jerk's convinced that since Alexandra is his wife he doesn't have to say anything that might hurt her."

"What?" she shouted. "They're divorced! Marital privilege doesn't cover his ass for this. That's bullshit."

Jansen cleared his throat. "Remember when I called before and said she was at the church?" He paused to let her think.

"You're f-ing kidding me!"

"I checked," Jansen reassured. "They got a marriage license Thursday morning—before Faraday even made it to the morgue. The waiting period was up today. She's a bitch, Detective, to the core. I told you."

"Just slow down, Jansen," she urged. "I know you can't stand her, but she didn't do it. Faraday killed himself and made it look like she did it." It felt strange to her to finally say it out loud, and obviously, it was just as strange to hear it; Jansen was speechless on the other end. "Just keep that to yourself for now. Let Vitale sit. I'll lock up here and be back to the station as soon as I can."

# Chapter 15

McCallister grabbed the tenth journal and quickly determined that it held no secrets. She counted and then seized the fortieth, noting that it contained papers from Faraday. He had taken it upon himself to draft his own autopsy report and to furnish a will, one she was hoping would take what he really loved into account. His sudden disregard for his orchids had perplexed her to no end. She took a cursory glance at the handwritten report, noting "suicide" as his cause of death. Then she saw Spangler's name in the will.

She shoved the whole journal into an evidence bag and did the same to the magazine and letter. As she was securing the guesthouse, the cell phone went off again, this time with the station telling her to call Douglas Penning.

"Detective," he began after she identified herself, "you said to call if had anything for you."

"What can I do for you, Mr. Penning?"

"Well, this is weird, but the wife got a delivery of flowers today. She assumed I was trying to get out of the doghouse or something, so she didn't think to look at the delivery tag. The flowers are for Thaddeus Frederick, but the address is definitely ours. I'm not sure what to do. The florist won't take them back because he says the address is correct. I'm not sure if I should try to go over to Frederick's house, what with the police tape and all, or if I—"

"That's okay, Mr. Penning. I'm right next door. I'll take care of it for you."

Within a minute of securing the scene and her evidence, she stood on the Penning's front porch with a basset hound sniffing her feet, a perturbed wife staring at her, and a fidgety man trying to protect her from both.

Penning handed her the bouquet of flowers along with the card. His wife swatted him a good one and said, "I should have known better than to figure you suddenly found a streak of romance after all these years." She turned and stomped back into the house.

McCallister gave him a quizzical look.

"Read the card," he said. Then his face went crimson.

The gift card was stock that read, "On your big day..." Then, in what she recognized as Faraday's penmanship, it said, "Turn up the heat." She quickly covered her mouth to stop the spontaneous laughter from erupting.

"Damn," he said defeatedly. "Now I am in the doghouse, and I didn't even do anything."

McCallister chuckled all the way to her car, tossing the flowers and the card onto the passenger seat. Faraday had actually given her a fairly simple clue, but in the wrong hands, it meant something completely different. She felt bad for Penning, but at least now she knew why Faraday had been so sure it was Wednesday. She wondered how long it would have taken her to find the magazine in the heat register with the aid of the clue. Regardless, she did not regret the hours she spent searching. In many ways, finding it on her own removed his cold hand from her shoulder, allowing her to steer again.

Despite the urgency to get to the station, she lit a cigarette and took a swig of her morning coffee, amazingly still warm from being in a closed car all day. Then she grabbed her cell and noted the time. It neared two, and that was hardly late enough to warrant a call to Holly about what time she'd be coming home. She used the guise, nonetheless, and texted, "Not sure how late. I need you. Bad!"

She smoked and waited. The eventual tone brought with it, "I'm right here, babe. Feel it?"

Indeed, she felt it—to the core of her. She relished it, and at the same time, it hurt. Unwittingly, Faraday had scathed her deepest vulnerability. She had seen death countless times—what it did to victims and those tormentedly left behind. When she saw it, she turned away and simply clung tighter to Holly, to what was dear, to what was life. But, Faraday made this one so personal that it felt like something inside had ripped loose, and she couldn't get it to stay in place. He taught her about the living death—the loss of oneself and the ability to distinguish what one loved. Oftentimes she had thought that if she lost Holly she would not want to be a part of this world anymore. But, that didn't mean just death anymore; it meant something as simple as forgetting that Holly's eyes were blue. She wanted to lay on top of her, memorize her for the millionth time, and then sob: for what she was blessed enough to have and just as terrified to lose.

She texted, "I do feel it, Hol. Thanks. I love you."

After taking a deep breath, she started her car and sped toward the station. A mere block later, the text tone came again. With an eye on the street and one on the screen, she read, "Need CFBR? too?" She pulled over and eagerly replied, "SOS CFBR ASAP." A soulful smiled swept over her face; she was revived.

A short time later, McCallister, Jansen, and Jessop sat in Captain Greeley's office.

"Faraday killed himself and set it up to make it look like his sister did it," she said very matter-of-factly. "I've got letters from him. He explained it all. It all matches up with what happened."

Greeley's jaw dropped. "Sharon is going to spit flaming turds at you, Laura." He paused to let his mind churn. "Why the hell would anyone do that?"

As she handed his final letter to Greeley, she explained that it was his last attempt to get Alexandra some help. "I really think he meant well, as twisted as this all is. I don't think he knew what else to do. He had Alzheimer's, and I don't think he believed for a second that she'd take care of him as the disease progressed. I think he also worried that as it progressed he wouldn't be able to care of her either. And speaking of taking care of…" She grabbed the evidence bag and removed the journal to get the will. "I want to know what he finally did with everything, since the other will was simply to create a motive."

As she fumbled with the papers, Greeley asked, "So why is Vitale still sitting here if we don't need him? Why don't you guys just cut him loose?"

"I still want to know why he lied, and why he'd marry her again," Jansen said.

Jessop proposed, "If Sinclair thought she about to go down for murder, maybe she just told him to lie about it to keep the heat off. She was grabbing at straws."

"Well, why was the cigarette case there to begin with?" Jansen argued. "Why lie? And why get married? What the hell did she not want him to say? She got Faraday to hand over all his money to her, and she goes and gives Vitale half through marriage? It doesn't make sense."

McCallister was barely listening. Instead, she read the will, dated the day after he signed the one with Dorsey. He named Dr. Spangler as executor and gave the house, his orchids, and $300,000 to the university. He gave Alexandra $150,000 per year from stocks, generously increasing the stipend if she received mental health treatment. He claimed to have changed the beneficiary on his life insurance policy to a nonprofit organization researching Alzheimer's, even though he had to have figured the claim would be denied with suicide as the cause of death. "Get this,"

McCallister said to them. "He left the Endicotts $75,000 'to help with new baby expenses' and because 'Jenny was always kind' to him."

A loud discussion commenced about how kind she truly was, but McCallister turned a deaf ear. Instead, she stared at the name suddenly looming off the paper: *Holly Crawford*. The sight of it made her stomach lurch. She read and realized that he had returned her painting to her and gave her the matching orchid in the greenhouse, both "to do with as she sees fit."

Abruptly, she stopped reading and handed the will to Jessop. "Find this lawyer so Spangler can start taking care of things."

Then she grabbed the autopsy report that Faraday had written. Her mind went to Shorty Malone and the grotesque things she believed should be rendered unthinkable by the mere act of breathing. As she began to read, she heard Greeley telling Jansen to let Vitale go. "No, Cap," she interrupted. "Jansen's right. I still want to know what his deal is. Maybe they're covering for something they did … like the always-kind Jenny was."

She resumed reading while Greeley yammered something about making sure everything was in order, giving Sharon Pierce a call, and getting the charges dropped. Jessop got up to leave so he could find the lawyer. Jansen was about to head out to check on Vitale and go over his notes.

But then, McCallister flew to a standing position. "Not so fast, guys," she said with a tone ominous enough to stop all activity. "I think we have a little problem."

They all looked at her. "What now?" Greeley asked.

"Seems Faraday's plan was a little different than how it all played out." She waved the paper at them and then read, "'This 73-year-old man died within 1-2 hours of injecting himself with' poison. It says there should be six to eight needle marks on the inside of his arm. His plan wasn't to drink it." She sat down and let her mind replay everything. "That's what they're hiding."

Greeley walked over to her, forcefully grabbed the paper from her hand, and read.

*Autopsy Report*

*Decedent: Tobias Albert Faraday, aka Thaddeus A. Frederick*

*DOB: January 12*

*DOD: April 7*

*Autopsy Foretold by: Tobias Albert Faraday, decedent*

132

*Identified by: Jenny Endicott, at scene*

*Manner of Death: Suicide*

*External Examination: Well-nourished white male*

*Gross Description*

*Brain: Some shrinkage to the temporal lobe due to early stage Alzheimer's Disease. This diagnosis can be verified by decedent's physician, Dr. Robert Roth. Decedent was treated using the alias of Thaddeus Faraday and did not visit his regular family physician due to privacy concerns.*

*GI Tract: Stomach and small intestine contain the decedent's last meal of choice: duck, roasted potatoes, and asparagus. Also present was Louis XIII de Rémy Martin, a cognac that the decedent, who had a poor sense of smell, always imagined tasted very good.*

*Extremities: 6-8 needle marks on the inside of left arm; skin under right-hand fingernails, matching sister's DNA*

*Other Lab Procedures: Toxicology, Photography*

*Disposition of Evidence*

*Toxicology: blood, vitreous, liver, bile, urine*

*Investigator: handwritten confession; syringe found on floor by fireplace with sister's fingerprints was not the one the decedent used; decedent destroyed the one he used by placing it into the fire.*

*Summary: This 73-year-old white male died within 1-2 hours of injecting himself 6-8 times with a mix of Malathion and Dichlorvo from his own stock. The multiple injections indicate that the decedent was intent on taking his life but was unsure about exactly how much was necessary. Overkill, hopefully.*

*Cause of Death: Respiratory arrest due to self-administered poison*

By the time, Greeley finished reading, McCallister had Hastings on the phone, asking him if there had been any needle marks on the body. After the third request for reassurance, he agreed to look again.

"I'll be right over." She said and the quickly stood to gather her things. "Jansen, Jessop, get over to the Faraday house right now," she ordered. "I want that box of syringes in the upstairs bedroom taken to the lab ASAP.

The old bottle of insulin, too. I'm going to have a chat with Hastings." She looked to Greeley. "And then, I'll talk to Sharon."

Half an hour later, she stood before Hastings as he read the report Faraday had written. "I'm sorry, Laura. They're just not there. I looked everywhere—with magnification. They're just not there. Besides, the poison was in his stomach contents; it was in the brandy snifter. He did not kill himself like he states here. Everything else is pretty close to spot-on, but he did *not* inject himself with poison."

A short time later she knew exactly what Greeley referred to as "flaming turds" being spit at her. Sharon Pierce was livid, and not in the way Hastings would use the word. She was raging angry.

"All you've done is given me enough reasonable doubt to sink every potential juror with an IQ over seven!" she wailed. "The sister did it! Slam-dunk. No, he killed himself! Case closed. No, wait! Maybe the sister really did it after all. How the hell can I convince a jury that she did it when there's just as much evidence that he did it—just not in the way he went into great detail to describe? Please!" She paused only to breathe and to use her renewed breath to laugh menacingly. "A man with a diagnosis of Alzheimer's? What's to say he didn't simply forget the finer details of his elaborate plan and drink the stuff?" She leaned over her desk, hands on her hips, and glared at her.

McCallister glared right back and calmly defended, "My job is to follow the evidence—wherever it leads. I don't get to pick and choose what works for you and what doesn't."

Surprisingly, the DA's anger seemed to subside, but McCallister suspected that it merely shape-shifted.

"You're right, Detective," she too easily conceded. "You don't get to pick and choose, but the goal of both our jobs is the same. That would be justice, if I remember correctly. If you don't give me what I need, you'll never see it … and neither will Sinclair *if* she did it." Her eyes widened.

McCallister stood, making sure she was eye-level with her, and then she said, "I'll get you what you need. Watch me!"

"Oh, I intend to, Detective. I'll be at your station in one hour." She glanced at her watch. "And I'll see to it that Dorsey and his client are there, ready and waiting for you. This one falls on you!" She waved her hand dismissively. "Nothing short of a confession will cut it, Detective."

McCallister bit her tongue to stop the slew of swear words standing at the ready. She knew the anger inside had been put there with intent, but that knowledge didn't lessen it. Rather, it intensified it and propelled her feet back to the station.

Purposefully, she made a considerable amount of noise as she entered Interrogation Room 3. With a big smile and an outstretched hand, she bellowed, "So you're the big man, huh? It's nice to meet you, Dominic." When he awkwardly extended his hand, she gave it a hearty shake. "I'm McCallister. I work here—obviously." She turned on the video recorder and took a seat, jolting the metal chair loudly as she did so. She drew a long labored breath and then said, "I'm supposed to be on vacation, but I've got a desk full of crap to take care of before the boss will let me out of here. So help me out, would you? This damn cigarette case. Would you please just tell me it's yours so I can just hand it over to you and close the damn file?" She looked at him expectantly.

He didn't answer. Instead, he shook his head.

"No, it's not yours, or no, you won't help me?" When he didn't answer, she looked at the cigarette case. "Your name's on it. The Faraday woman's name's on it. You're obviously a big man. And then, there's your print. Now, maybe I haven't been on the job all that long, but that sure says to me that the damn thing is yours. Would you please just cop to it so I can get out of here?"

He still didn't answer.

"It looks awfully expensive, too," she said, turning the case to look at it from every angle. "Ah, but you're a rich man again, what with marrying the last Faraday heir and everything." She smiled at him. "Oh, is that what it is? It doesn't mean anything to you anymore? Shit, on a cop's pay, I could— Never mind."

"Take it," he dared. "Slip it in your pocket and go on your goddamn vacation."

She shook her head. "Nah, I'd never get away with it." She tilted her head toward the camera. "Besides, they tape everything. You can't even sneak a smoke in this joint without somebody knowing." She shook her head again. "And I sure need a smoke. You smoke?" With a laugh, she corrected, "That was a stupid question. Of course, you smoke. You have an expensive cigarette case. What the hell would you put in it if you didn't?"

She watched him fidget. Always talk about smoking when a smoker's locked in a non-smoking room; she knew from experience how nasty that was. Then she leaned in close to him and whispered, "So did that Faraday woman ask you to marry her or did you pop the big question?" He glared at her, and she said, "I'm sorry; that was awfully personal. It's just that she's got a reputation. I mean … you know."

"No, I don't know," he said with an angry squint of his eyes.

"Well, somebody I work with said they heard her say that guys were all the same, that if she yanked in the right place, they'd do anything she wanted them to do."

Vitale looked disgusted and incensed. He scowled at McCallister,

135

who nodded her head enthusiastically and assured, "She did! I swear." She tilted her head to the recorder again. "Trust me. She said it, and somebody's sure as hell got it on tape. Did she yank you, Dominic?"

"That's disgusting," he snarled and leaned away from her.

"It is, isn't it? I'm sorry. If I were you, I wouldn't want to admit it either," she agreed. Quickly, she leaned in closer. "And who put this crap in your head that just because you're married you don't have to say anything against her? That is like so not true. Did the Faraday woman tell you that? Man, I hope you didn't pay a shyster lawyer for that crap advice! Oh, I keep forgetting." She stopped to laugh. "You don't have to worry about money anymore now that the old guy's dead."

"Detective, you're out of line."

"Yes, you're right. I am. I'm sorry. I'm overworked. I need vacation." She hung her head. "This was just supposed to be about the stupid cigarette case. Just tell me the truth, man, and we can end this. Then we can both go."

"Fine!" he spat. "Yes, it's mine!"

"Then why the hell did you lie about it? Crap advice again?"

"No!" he said angrily. "You people made a big deal out of it! You arrested her; her lawyer said not to say anything. I shouldn't have lied. I should have said nothing, but now you know. Alex forgot it at Tobias' house. That's all. Now, we can just drop it. I did something wrong, not Alex. It was stupid." He slid his chair back. "Are we done?"

"Well, see, Dominic, we would have been done." She banged her fist on the table in frustration. She quickly scanned Alexandra's apartment and Faraday's house in her mind. "It would have been over, but you had to go and cover a lie by telling another lie. Shit, I'm never going to get out of here!" An exaggerated sigh made its way out of her mouth.

"I didn't lie!" he defended, sitting up straight in his chair.

With yet another sigh, McCallister put the side of her head on the table. "Alex doesn't smoke. See, Dominic, if you keep lying to me and this shit doesn't add up in the blessed file and with all these video recorders recording every second of every single day of my frickin' life, I'll never get the hell out of here." She paused briefly and then continued, "Alex doesn't smoke, but she took your cigarette case to her brother's house the night he was murdered. See what I mean? How the hell do I write that in the file and have it make sense?" She sat upright and looked at him with pleading eyes. "You seem like a nice man, Dominic. Please, I just want to get out of here!"

"Well, what the hell do you want me to say?"

"The truth would be a nice place to start … I mean at least the stuff that won't hurt her … at least until you stop believing the crap advice you got about being able to protect her."

"Fine! What do you want to know that has nothing to do with her? Ask."

"Cool," she acknowledged with a broad smile. "Like where'd you lay low during the five-day waiting period after you got the marriage license? Somewhere posh?"

"My brother has a cabin up north," he said with a quizzical look.

"Cool," she said again. "And did it bother you to watch Faraday writhe in pain, dying there, while you smoked your cigarettes?"

"Detective—"

"Did the cigarettes calm you—"

"Detective—"

"Did it make you feel bad that—"

"Detective—

Quickly and loudly, she shouted, "There was no ashtray there, big man! Did you have to toss your ashes over him, dying there, to hit the fireplace? I don't think I could have—"

"Detective!" he yelled so loudly that it seemed to make the room resonate. "I think I want a—"

"Cigarette! Me frickin', too! I'll see what I can do."

In two seconds flat, he was alone in the room, rubbing his hands on his thighs and occasionally glancing to the video recorder.

# Chapter 16

McCallister stood in the hall and looked at her watch. She had twenty minutes before she needed to worry about Sinclair and Dorsey. A nicotine fit raged. She was about to head to her desk for her jacket when Greeley's head poked out the door adjacent to the interrogation room.

"Have one in your hideout on the roof. It's quicker," he said.

"You're not supposed to know about that!" McCallister exclaimed.

"I wasn't always a captain," he replied. "Besides, the press will be all over downstairs once they figure out Sinclair's on her way."

Suddenly, Sharon Pierce's head appeared next to Greeley's. "Can I join you, Detective?" When McCallister cautiously nodded, she added, "Then I can give you some better-than-crap advice about spousal privilege." Her tone bordered on haughty.

McCallister chuckled to herself as they turned down the hall. "I don't want better-than-crap, Sharon. Crap works rather well in there. All I have to do is make sure I don't violate anybody's rights or knock anybody's block off."

When they reached the roof, McCallister lit up, and Sharon advised, "I need what you get in there, though. Any mistakes could have a negative effect on testimony. With the position you've suddenly thrust me in, I need there to be no question about admissibility. So you need to know—"

"Well, this is what I do know," McCallister interrupted, refusing to be intimidated or buy into the notion that this was somehow her fault. "There are two kinds of privilege. One survives divorce. They other doesn't. So they were obviously worried about the one that doesn't: adverse testimony. But, you could always argue that they weren't married the night of the murder, that the marriage was a ruse. Then again, the whole caboodle goes out the window if they were co-conspirators. But, you want a confession and not one flipping on the other; that'll make it cleaner."

To McCallister's amazement, the DA released a hearty laugh. "Okay, you already have better-than-crap. I'll just shut up." In an instant, though, she reverted to her despot ways. "You know what I need, Detective. Get it!" She retreated through the door.

McCallister shook her head and enjoyed a few drags of her cigarette. Then, shouting voices in the distance seized her attention. She went to look over the edge and watched reporters in the parking lot flying out of vehicles to pelt Alexandra Sinclair with questions. Dorsey had her by the arm and briskly escorted her into the building.

With the prey now in her sights, she headed back to her desk to review the crime scene photos, making sure that there really wasn't an ashtray in Faraday's house. Then she headed into Interrogation Room 2.

Upon entry, she pleasantly smiled at both of them. "Congratulations on your nuptials, Mrs. Sinclair." She paused and then genuinely corrected, "Oh, I'm sorry. That would be Mrs. Vitale."

Alexandra faked a smile at her.

McCallister turned on the video camera and took a seat across the table from them, her back to the door. She looked intently at Alexandra and then turned her gaze on Dorsey. "If you prefer, Mrs. Vitale, we can talk alone. I'm not sure if Mr. Dorsey is a Neanderthal or not."

"Good try, Detective," Dorsey spouted, "but I'll be staying."

"That's fine, just fine with me, Mr. Dorsey," she replied with a smile and then fixed her eyes on Alexandra. "Is Dominic a Neanderthal?"

"No. Actually, he's a very good man," Alexandra quickly answered.

"Better than the first time you married him, I hope. Oh, but then, it's entirely possible he left you, isn't it?" She shook her head and hurriedly continued before Dorsey had a chance to release the rebuke he was assembling. "Would you care to tell me why your big man's cigarette case was at the scene of your brother's murder, Alexandra? That way I can make sure your story matches what he already told me."

With a boastful tone, she said, "I don't have to answer your questions, Detective."

"No. No, you don't. You are quite right about that." She vigorously nodded her head. "You're a tough one, Mrs. Vitale. Let me think. I'm sure I can come up with something we can safely talk about." She put her elbow to the table and her head to her hand while she made a series of "hmm" sounds. Raising her eyes slightly, she watched Alexandra give Dorsey a look that berated the futile attempt to get her to talk.

McCallister stalled for several long minutes and then abruptly sat straight up to exclaim, "Oh, I know what I wanted to ask you!" She smiled and exuded a sense of triumph. "Your brother! Tobias! Did Tobias have a sudden interest in your syringes lately?"

Alexandra squinted her eyes, first with suspicion and then with remembrance. She recalled, "Yes, as a matter of fact, he did. A couple of weeks ago. He said it would be easier to treat his damn orchids without hurting their leaves ... or something simpleminded like that."

"Did you show him how to use them? Did he have you fill one with whatever he treats them with?"

"Yes," she acknowledged and then suspicion returned. "What does this have to do with anything?"

McCallister waved a dismissive hand. "Just items in his house that we need to account for." She then asked about his recent moods, and Alexandra reported that he actually seemed happier in recent weeks. "How did he broach the subject of estate planning with you?"

Alexandra laughed. "Careful, Detective, you're starting to make it seem like perhaps you believe me. You wouldn't want to weaken the big motive you think I have." After McCallister assured her that she believed Faraday raised the issue and Dorsey gave her a nod, she continued, "He did bring it up, not me. He said he wanted to make sure he had everything in order and did the right thing. I simply told him that the money belonged in the family, and I was all that was left of it. The university did not need the money."

"Mrs. Vitale, did he give you any indications that something was wrong with him, something that made him think he might be dying soon?"

With a cold stare, Alexandra simply said, "No."

"Oh, I don't mean that he knew you were going to kill him," she clarified with a smile. "I mean: Did he give you any hints that something was wrong—physically?"

She continued to glare at her. "I'm not going to answer questions when you phrase things like that. I did not kill him."

McCallister looked quizzically at Dorsey. "Do you think she killed him, Mr. Dorsey?"

"You know better than to ask me something like that!" he spat. "And *I* don't have to answer your questions either. I'm the lawyer not the accused! Why isn't the DA here? She'd never get away with posing questions like this."

"I'm not sure where she is, come to think of it," she replied. "So you don't have to answer my questions. Alexandra doesn't have to answer my questions. How about the talkative big man in the next room? Did you tell him he doesn't have to answer questions either? Seems you all have something to protect. But, Dorsey, I don't think you're trying to protect either of them. I think—"

"That's out of line, Detective!"

141

"I get so tired of hearing how I'm out of line all the time! Jesus!" She shook her head. "See, Mr. Dorsey, you're executor of the estate ... at least according to the will you have in your possession. No? Millions at your disposal—well, if Alexandra goes to prison anyway."

"That's insane. I want Pierce in here!"

"I'll see if I can find her," she said but made no effort whatsoever to do so. Intently, she stared into Alexandra's eyes. "Alex, Dorsey *is* a Neanderthal. He'll leave you high and dry while he smiles and says he's defending you. Has he ever even handled a murder case before? I honestly don't know, but I do know one thing. He'll abandon you. He'll leave you, Alex—"

"This interview is over, Detective!" He stood and pulled his client by the arm. "Alex, we're leaving."

McCallister kept shouting Alexandra's name until she made eye contact. "Alex, did you know he told me your disposition was as sour as a lemon?"

Alexandra stared at her briefly, and then her eyes shot to Dorsey. "Did you?"

"No! Don't listen to her. And for God's sake, don't say anything! I know what I'm doing."

McCallister laughed and challenged, "Come on, Dorsey! You remember saying it. Don't lie to her. You remember. We were at that little deli downtown. You and me. You were eating turkey on whole wheat, but you couldn't finish it. I had coffee. You remember! You said her thumb was as green as a lemon and her deposition just as sour. I thought it was funny at the time, but now that you're defending—"

"Alex, let's go!"

Again, McCallister verbally blocked the path to the door. "I swear, Mrs. Vitale! That's what he said. He's a Neanderthal just like the rest of them. He'll leave you. He'll leave you ... high and dry. Mark my words. He won't defend you. He doesn't care about you. He wants control of the money. He'll let you get convicted. And then, he'll leave. Mark my words!"

"Alex, I mean it. I'm ordering you to leave. *Now!*"

Alexandra flew to her feet. "You're ordering me? Who pays your goddamn bill, Arlen? You son-of-a-bitch, you work for me! You do what *I* say!"

"Yeah, sit down, Dorsey, you Neanderthal!" McCallister yelled. "Alex is in charge! Not you! She can make her own decisions."

"I'll have your badge, Detective!" he seethed, his neck bulging to the point where his green tie looked like a noose.

"And I'll report you to the bar. You're putting your own interests before your client's." She looked to Alexander. "He wants you to go to prison so he can control the money, the family money, the money that should go to you!" She shot a look to Dorsey. "And then you're just going to leave her! You don't care about her, only yourself." Her eyes returned to Alexandra. "Alex, he doesn't care about you. He'll get you convicted. Mark my words. He's going to leave you, Alex! You're not just going to let him leave you, are you, Alex?"

A nasty mix of fear and anger swept over Alexandra's face. With a sound that seemed to shake the foundation of the building itself, her hand slapped Dorsey's face. "You son-of-a-bitch! Get the hell out of my sight!"

He seized his briefcase from the table and shouted, "Fine, Alex. You're on your own!"

As he flew through the opening door, Alexandra yelled to him, "I've done pretty goddamn well on my own, you son-of-a-bitch!"

McCallister stood and looked directly into Alexandra's face. "Boy, you are one strong woman, Mrs. Vitale! I really respect that." She watched Alexandra's chest heave and her hands shake. "And you're probably strong enough to hear what I've got to tell you about Dominic. See, he's a Neanderthal, too. As soon as I told him what prison time he'd get for being an accessory to this mess, he just caved ... *just caved* ... like a stupid little man. I'm so sorry, Alex. I really thought he was a tough one who would stand by you, but he left you, too ... high and dry."

"He wouldn't!" Alex screamed. "He helped me! He wouldn't turn on me like that! You're lying!" Then she turned the fear and anger directly on McCallister. "You're lying!"

"Oh, I wish I were, Alex. I'm very sorry." She moved her hand as if to reach out and offer comfort, and then at the last second she pulled back. "He might have tried to help, but come on! The stupid man left his cigarette case right there for the Neanderthal cops to find! He might as well have left a signed confession. I don't think the stupid cops would even have figured out if that cigarette case hadn't been sitting on the bar right next to your tote. You came back to get it for him, didn't you? Cleaning up after a stupid man! Right where he left it, but the Neanderthal cops had it by then. Right where he left it. And why was he so stupid not to grab your things? Your tote? Your coat? Your umbrella? He started to; I'll give him that, but then he left it all. Not even where they belonged. Why by the bar—like it didn't even matter? Why? Because he's stupid! For God's sake, aren't there any smart men in this world, ones who won't leave things, ones who won't leave at all, ones who won't leave you?"

Alexandra just glared at her, and McCallister could see the humanity draining from her eyes. "I mean really! It's pouring rain, and he leaves your goddamn umbrella by the bar! Your coat on a stool? Typical man. Stupid man. Goddamn Neanderthals. And Tobias… God, let's don't even get started on that stupid man!" She shoved her metal chair into the table with a bang that startled Alexandra into movement. Loudly, she fired questions at her, "Why did he forget your umbrella? Why did he just leave it like that? Wasn't it pouring rain outside? Was he that stupid? A woman needs an umbrella. Didn't he give a shit? Did he all of a sudden think he didn't have to do what you told him to do? Didn't he remember you were in charge? Why wasn't he thinking about you and your needs? He left you high and dry, too! Stupid goddamn Neanderthal! Stupid man! What the hell was he thinking?"

Very calmly, too calmly for McCallister's comfort level, Alexandra said, "He heard a siren."

McCallister shoved her chair again. She banged her fists on the table. "Alex!" she yelled. "Was he stupid and afraid of a goddamn siren, too? Tobias was dead. Why the hell didn't you both just leave! Just take the stuff and leave! Just leave! Just leave! Your dear brother had already left you! He was dead!"

And then, McCallister imagined the sound of an oak tree being cracked in two. Alexander wailed, "He wasn't goddamn dead! The son-of-a-bitch wouldn't die!" Her eyes grew inhumanly wide, and she shrieked, "He moaned! He cried! He begged! He threw up! He shook! God, he shook! It was the most fucking disgusting thing I have ever seen in my whole goddamn life! The son-of-a-bitch did everything but die!" Rage and panic contorted her face. She raised her hands and pivoted side to side, looking for something on which to unleash. Her thick, trembling hands seized the table edge. She hoisted and pitched the table as hard as she could.

McCallister bolted backwards and narrowly missed being hit by the overturning table. With a clap, it landed on its side on the bare floor, but louder still, she shouted, "Alex, why wouldn't he die? Why wouldn't the son-of-a-bitch die? Because Dominic didn't give him enough?"

Alexandra suddenly froze in place, and as though a switch had been flipped, she laughed maniacally. "Dominic? That coward! He couldn't even kill him when he was half-dead. Then he fucks up and leaves everything there! God damn him! Runs like a fucking coward when he hears a siren that wasn't even coming for him. Yeah, he'll fix it. He'll take care of it! He'll fucking take care of it all right!"

"Why wouldn't the son-of-a-bitch die, Alex?" she yelled even louder. "Why wouldn't Tobias die? Why wouldn't your brother die? How much did you give him? Did *you* fuck up?"

She glared at McCallister again, her eyes black with rage, the switch

144

having flipped again. "*I* didn't fuck up! I don't fuck up! That glass was nearly full! I don't fuck up! *You* fucked up, you son-of-a-bitch!"

"How did I fuck up, Alex?"

But Alex didn't answer. Instead, she snatched the chair next to her and flung it full force with guttural scream.

McCallister avoided the brunt of it, but the hinges smacked her forehead loudly. Losing her balance, she fell backwards to the floor, stunned. Her head slowly began to bleed. Before she could even get her bearings, the door burst open and Greeley and Jessop started methodically moving toward Alexandra.

"Leave, Neanderthals! Leave!" McCallister spat at them. She unsteadily rose and neared them. Acting as though she was shoving them out the door, she handed her gun off to Greeley, yelling, "Men leave! Stupid men leave! *Leave!*" She slammed the door and leaned her back onto it. Willfully, she took a deep breath, trying to make the stars in her head burn out. She breathed deeply once more, and then in a calmer voice, she asked, "How did I fuck up, Alex?"

But she simply stared at her, maybe through her.

McCallister realized that Alexandra's rage had dissipated in the violent outburst and the subsequent interruption. But she also understood that what she had gotten from her wasn't as clean as what the DA needed. From her distance she desperately tried to get a feel for where Alexandra had gone. Had she plummeted over the edge, or had she landed back at square one where belligerence and denial hailed?

Sensing stupor more than anything, she began moving toward her, carefully and quietly pushing chairs aside and finally pulling the table away so it didn't block her access to Alexandra.

Softly she said, "We sure made a mess of the room. I'll make those men clean up after us." She cautiously made the last few steps to her and held handcuffs out in front of her. "I'm sorry, but I have to put these on you. Next time someone comes in here, it'll be with guns drawn. We don't want that, do we, Alexandra?"

Alexandra didn't resist. She merely stood there with the same blank look on her face. McCallister cuffed her and almost soothingly asked, "Did you plan to kill him, Alex?"

Slowly, she shook her head. "No. It just happened."

"How?"

"He kept talking about leaving me. He said he had to leave. He was sorry he had to leave." She paused briefly and then said, "People don't leave me, Detective. I tell them when to leave."

"So you were angry ... scared maybe."

"He made such a big deal about the bottle of poison. It was all I

145

could think about. I just did it, but I had no idea it was going to be like that."

"Did Dominic help you?"

"No! No. I called him after Tobias wouldn't die. He came over ... yelled at me ... told me to leave. Said he'd take care of it." She shook her head again as if trying to detach the images there. "I really didn't know he'd suffer like that. I didn't." Then, she looked at McCallister. "Detective, what am I going to do without my brother?" Instantly, she began to sob.

McCallister led her to the observation mirror and raised her fist to rap on it, but suddenly she stopped. Anger roiled within her. She wanted to light into her with words about evil and selfishness and secrets and sins—and then about love and loyalty. Instead, the clouds in a dead man's eyes floated through her mind. She reminded herself that it had to come down to those clouds in his eyes, that it had to begin and end with compassion and requital for the victim. The system would mete out justice to the perpetrator, but for this precise moment, it wasn't about Alexandra, and it wasn't about her. It was about Tobias, and she knew, she knew very well what he wanted, even now. She remembered his words in that meticulous penmanship, "This must work, Detective. This is my very last shot."

She swallowed hard, rapped on the window, and said, "Alex, I know Tobias loved you very much, and all he really wanted was for you to get some help, to find some peace. Wherever he is right now, I'm sure that if you did that, it would please him ... even after this ... even if just to make up for this."

Jansen and Jessop entered, and McCallister handed Alexandra off to them and to the system.

# Chapter 17

"Congratulations, Detective," Sharon Pierce said with a wide smile as she and Greeley entered the interrogation room. "You did a very good job. Thank you."

McCallister stared at her briefly and then very coldly said, "Do *not* congratulate me for what I just did to another human being."

Greeley swiftly walked between them and took McCallister by the arm. "Come on, Laura. I want somebody to look at that nasty wound of yours." He led her out of the room.

In the hall, she moved her hand to touch her throbbing head. It smarted, and her hand returned with blood. "It's just a scratch, Cap," she lied. "No big deal."

"Don't give me crap, Laura. You're bleeding," he asserted. "I've got an EMT on the way. For once, you're going to listen to me."

"Please, Cap. Just give me ten minutes to myself. Then you can do whatever the hell you want." She looked at him and smiled. "Please? I just need a smoke and a chance to clear my head. I promise. Whatever you want after that, I'll just keep my mouth shut."

"Well, just seeing that might be worth it," he retorted. "But go easy, and put something on it to stop the bleeding. If you get dizzy, sit down! And if you're not back in ten minutes, I *will* hunt you down!"

"Yes, sir!" She feigned a salute and then slowly headed up the stairs, sensing Greeley's watchful eyes monitoring her every step.

Once outside, she greedily breathed the chilly air into her. She paused to appraise and then smiled when she noted that the gnawing knot in her stomach no longer existed. She sat and leaned against the rooftop's outer ledge. After lighting a cigarette, she grabbed her cell phone, knowing she owed one big favor. "Hey, chink repairer, there will be a bragging district attorney out in front of the station in no more than ten minutes. Be ready!"

Then, she put her aching head back and concentrated on nothing but the darkening blue sky. Instantly, her mind conjured up an image of Albert Regis, leaning against a shed, watching his stresses float away in a whirl of white smoke. She visualized her own tensity leaving, companioned by every facet of the investigation. And then, she let Albert go, sending him on his way with all the Faraday secrets and sins in tow. She closed her eyes and breathed deeply, acknowledging that her own sin in all of it would need to be faced if the letting go was to be clean—when she was ready.

Her cigarette reached its end, and she headed downstairs to discover a crowd at her desk.

An EMT pointed to her chair and said, "Have a seat, Detective, so I can check you over."

"For shit's sake, it was a folding chair not a chaise lounge!"

"So much for keeping her mouth shut," Greeley said, defeatedly handing Jansen a five-dollar bill.

Smiling broadly, Jansen smiled shoved the cash into his pocket.

McCallister's mouth hung open in utter disbelief. "You bet on it? Jesus, you guys!"

"Now, quiet, Laura. Everybody's been waiting for the day when you finally get your head examined," Greeley roared.

Laughter erupted, the healthy kind that blew off steam, the kind that cleansed the body of the depravity it had just brushed up against. Maybe it was a cop thing. Maybe it was purely human. Whatever it was, it felt like an urgent need.

Fifteen minutes and two refusals to get checked at the hospital later, McCallister was advised to take it easy for a couple of days, report any dizziness or blurred vision, and refrain from driving. Her forehead sported a large piece of gauze that covered a butterfly bandage. She felt rather foolish sitting there with everyone staring at her.

Greeley spoke up when the EMT left. "I do not want to see you until a week from Monday."

"Because of this? That's insane! It's nothing! Honest!"

"Two days for the head, and next week for the vacation you've got coming. And if I see your face at a murder scene, it had better be on the corpse," he spouted and then returned her gun to her. "We'll take care of Vitale and the reports. Now, get out of here! One of these guys will drive you home."

"No! I'm not an eight-year-old. I can get home by myself," she argued. When he glared at her, she conceded, "Fine! I'll get my own damn ride. Leave me alone now. Please!"

Begrudgingly, she grabbed her cell. She was not about to call Holly; she'd worry needlessly. Instead, she called Kate, and when it was clear to her that the press' feeding frenzy had just ended, she asked for a ride. "But would you sneak me out the side door? ... I really don't want to see any of your snap-happy colleagues."

She got into Kate's car to receive a slew of questions about her bandaged forehead and her bloody shirt, none of which she would answer. Instead, she begged for a chance to run into the House of Lee for the expected dinner—for Holly, for the one she could not wait to hold close. After losing the argument about whether a bloody woman lent to the ambience of a restaurant, she petulantly sat in the car while Kate made the run for her.

Twenty minutes later, Kate pulled into the driveway. As McCallister grabbed the bag and began to exit, Kate said, "Whatever you did to get a confession, good job. But, to tell you the truth, I was hoping to suck another few months of reporting out of this during the trial." She laughed. "And I think I'm going to miss huddling in the alley with you, letting you steal my coffee. But regardless, good work!" She paused and then looked her squarely in the eyes. "This one was tough. Take care of my bud, will you?"

McCallister smiled and then made her way to the front door. She did her best to walk into the house sideways, wanting the warmth of an embrace before the heat of questioning. It worked splendidly: Holly lunged at her and gave her a soul-saving hug. When she pulled back for the welcoming kiss, however…

"Oh my God, Laura, what happened?" Immediately, her eyes welled with tears, and she gently touched McCallister's cheek. "Are you okay, babe? What the hell happened?"

"I'm fine, Hol. Really," she reassured. "My ego's hurt worse than my head. ... Honey, I got clunked a good one by a woman more than twice my age. Not pretty."

Holly laughed. "We'll work on your story tomorrow, babe. How tall did you say the guy was? Six five?" She kissed her and asked whether she needed to go to the emergency room.

McCallister explained that she had been checked out already but slyly added, "I think they're worried about a concussion, Hol. He told me I have to spend two whole days in bed ... completely naked so nothing constricts the blood flow to my noggin ... oh, and I shouldn't be left alone for even a minute." She drew her near. "Can we manage that, hon?"

"Oh, I'm sure we can, babe. Don't you worry your clunked little head," Holly said very seriously. She gave her another kiss and then pulled away with the House of Lee bag. "Let's get you cleaned up and comfy. Then, after we eat, I'll make a few calls. I'm sure we can find you a big, mean, ugly, smelly nurse who just *loves* to give sponge baths." She grabbed her by the hand and led her down the hall. Rolls of cathartic laughter led the way.

For the next two days, McCallister did nothing but decompress and let time heal both heart and forehead. She didn't fill Holly in on any of the details of the case, leaving that to Kate's thorough articles in the newspaper that hit the doorstep each day. She didn't even tell her about the will, leaving that to Spangler in his capacity as executor. Her muteness met with respect. Holly was that way; she didn't needlessly pry, and yet, she always had an attentive ear at the ready.

In McCallister's own way, she simply did her best to move on, to make sure she never again looked into Tobias Faraday's cloudy eyes or felt his deathly cold hand on her shoulder. It was over, and yet, that part deep inside her that had ripped loose proved unwilling to heal. An inner wound festered, something that a butterfly bandage could not reach to hold in place. When she seemed nearly to touch it herself, she recoiled in fear.

While McCallister took it easy, Holly scrambled to get her work out of the way. Clearing her following week's schedule would allow them to take another stab at vacation. She worked madly, and repeatedly, McCallister found herself seated on the patio watching her through the studio's windows. She stared. She memorized. She marveled. She loved from afar. And mostly, she felt tears rise in her throat, ones that seemed so big and powerful she was certain they would choke her to death if they rose too high.

On one such occasion, she had just received a smile from Holly when suddenly the tears proved unswallowable. Holly turned back to her easel, and McCallister closed her eyes, daring to imagine the day when she could no longer see her, when she would never see her again. Her eyes shot open when pain and tears erupted full force. As if sensing it, Holly abruptly turned to face her with an eerily solemn expression. Instantly, McCallister raised the book she held and pretended to read. Within a matter of seconds, however, Holly towered over her. She knelt and pulled her into an embrace. She asked nothing, and instead, she simply held her, giving permission in a way that caused McCallister finally to release a hoard of emotion.

Soon, Holly pulled away slightly and asked, "Laura, what's wrong?"

McCallister shook her head and replied, "I just love you. That's all." She clung tighter.

"Since when does that hurt? Why would that hurt?" When McCallister didn't answer, she pulled completely away from her and implored, "Babe, please talk to me."

McCallister sniffed, took a deep breath, and tried to give a voice to the excruciating pain inside her. "What I feel for you, honestly, just overwhelms me sometimes. I love you so much. ... When I imagine losing you, it just feels like I'm dying inside, like I want to die inside. I can't stand it!" She wept uncontrollably, pulling her near and clutching as if life depended upon it.

Holly held her for several minutes, and then she sat on the ground in front of her. She looked into her eyes. "You're breaking the promise, Laura ... but you know that, otherwise, you would have told me." A gentle smile spread across her face. "Do you remember the promise?"

McCallister could recall the exact second that promise came into being. She always did; she always would. They had dated for over a year, and then one night, they made the commitment to spend the rest of their lives together. What followed was their first experience of physical intimacy with each other, savored without once breaking the intense gaze between them. They both believed that the unyielding peering in melded their souls, rendering them incomplete without the other. And in that fusion, they promised always to keep their eyes riveted to each other. There was no past; there was no moment beyond—only now and that giddy desperation to feel completed by the other. It was as though the first time they made love, in a way that transcended the mere physical, they just simply never stopped. Satiation became the enemy not the goal. Desire and the love they felt for each other existed only in the now—where they vowed to reside together.

"Of course, I remember the promise, Hol," McCallister affirmed. Then, she shook her head in defeat, finally admitting her own secret, her own sin. "I looked away, hon. I flinched. ... It wasn't intentional. ... It's like my head was forced in a different direction, if that makes any sense. ... Now it's as though I can't stop looking at what I saw, feeling what I felt when I imagined you not with me. It kills me, but I can't stop looking! And what I feel makes me want to just curl up and die. I flinched." Again, she shook her head and then tearfully lowered it. "I'm sorry, Holly."

"Babe, I'm not looking for an apology. Just for a way for you not to hurt." She grabbed McCallister's hands, kissed each one, and then wove her fingers into them. "I know I've got it a lot easier than you do. Your job makes you have to look at all the cruel things in life. Me, I paint what I want; I see what I want. If I painted evil all day, I'd probably flinch, too. But, you have to find away to stop looking away from *here*, Laura. Every time you go off into a made-up future, we're not together. You're bringing about exactly what you're afraid of. Thinking about losing me *is* losing me, babe. You have to love me here, in the present, in this very moment. And *this* is loving me." She put her hands on the sides of McCallister's face and enticed her to look into her eyes. "Look at me. I'm right here, babe—not there. I'm here now, and I love you. If you can't stay here with me, tell me—please just tell me. I promise I can bring you back." She returned to a kneeling position and wrapped her arms tightly around her. "Now get every last smidgen of that crap out of you. It doesn't belong here."

McCallister cried, and yet for the first time, she knew the well of tears had a bottom; she would not choke with its rising. Every time she felt Holly's hand stroking her head, there were fewer tears. Every time she inhaled the scent of her, it emptied further. The present was no longer blurred at the bottom of the pool. And without a reservoir of tears giving it buoyancy, the piece of her that had ripped loose slumped in submission and reattached.

———

Monday began the first official day of their vacation. They spent the entire day in bed, sprawled out on luxury sheets, simply wallowing in utter togetherness. They saw the sun gleaming outside. They listened to the ocean waves gently crashing and then pulling back. They heard the sounds of gulls. And at five o'clock, they heeded a knock at the door.

"Room service!" McCallister announced. She quickly grabbed a quarter from the nightstand, flipped it, and called heads just in time to see tails.

"Shit!" Holly said with a giggle. She flew into her robe and grabbed money from the wallet in her purse.

Moments later, she returned, flung a pizza box at McCallister, and disrobed. As she slid back into bed, she ordered, "Do not let any of those disgusting anchovies even look at my mushrooms." She refilled their wine glasses and traded one for a slice of pizza from the fish-less half.

They kissed, feasted, laughed, and repeated.

Half an hour later, they were in each other arms, concentrating on the sounds and feeling quite content to return to simple wallowing.

Then, in all her whining glory, Holly declared, "Babe, I'm sick of Maine. Don't these birds ever shut up? Can we go somewhere else?"

McCallister started laughing, and it seemed to be a contagion that quickly infected the both of them. Shaking with laughter, she leaned to the nightstand. "Where do you want to go, Hol? You name it; I'll take you there."

"Well, suggest some place."

"Okay, let's see. … How about Jamaica?"

"No! That's just more birds and waves. How about something

inland?"

"Oh, here we go! How about a summer night in, say ... I don't know ... Idaho?"

"Idaho? What's in Idaho besides potatoes?"

"You and me. As long as we're together, it doesn't matter where we are. Isn't that what we said?"

"Yes, but Idaho?" She laughed hysterically. "Okay. Fine. Let's go to Idaho."

McCallister grabbed a CD from the collection on the nightstand and tossed it to Holly, who promptly removed "Relaxation: Sounds of the Ocean" and replaced it with "Relaxation: Summer Night Sounds." She hit the play button, and the two curled into each other.

"Oh Jesus! Crickets!" Holly soon roared. She sat up and grabbed McCallister's hand. "Let's go sit on the patio and pretend we're vacationing on the deck of the *Titanic*. I'm going to want to jump after all these damn crickets and birds."

McCallister pulled her back down. "How about we just admit that home is where we want to be? I just want to hear you beside me. Nothing more. I could very easily listen to nothing else, forever."

Holly contributed the first sounds to their new collection when she kissed McCallister and simultaneously whacked the CD player.

# Epilogue

Three months passed in the sleepy little city while McCallister enjoyed what she called the doldrums of burglary and arson.

It was a sunny Tuesday when Holly picked her up from a slow day at work for an early dinner. As they drove, she explained that they had an errand to run beforehand. Soon, her little red car skirted the curb in front of East Park Nursing Center.

"Oh shit! Are you having me committed to the old folks' home, Hol?" McCallister asked as Holly turned off the ignition.

"Not quite yet," she joked. "I just want to show you something. Come on!"

They entered the facility, and suddenly Holly's name was spoken by at least fifteen different smiling and eager faces. McCallister found herself very perplexed, thinking perhaps her lover lived a double life. Holly went from person to person, clutching hands and greeting each by name.

"Everybody, this is Laura," she announced. Then, she spun toward a grinning man in a wheelchair and said, "She's a cop, Chester, so do not flirt with me, or she will bust your chops!" She laughed, and he joined her after doing a darn-it snap of his fingers. "And, Laura, these sweet people are my new friends."

After warm introductions, Holly took McCallister by the arm and led her down the hall and into a sunroom. She pointed to the wall, and there hung the orchid painting from Faraday's sitting room. Then she pointed to the windowsill, and there sat the orchid from the greenhouse. "Tobias said I could do as I saw fit. Both of those things here—in a place that helps people with Alzheimer's—that's what I thought was fitting. Those things don't belong with us. Let these guys enjoy them."

McCallister's eyes welled with tears. "You have a good heart, hon." She found herself very relieved that Holly had chosen to let go of what Faraday had given her. She had told her she would support whatever decision she made, and she would have. But this one felt right.

Holly smiled at her. "I need you to look closely at the painting, Laura. Memorize it."

Again, McCallister met with confusion. Holly gently steered her in front of the painting. "See anything different, Detective?"

McCallister smirked at her challenge and studied. Eventually, she said with a gasp, "Oh my God, Hol, you didn't!" She moved closer, zeroing in on the white stick containing the orchid's code. In the bottom corner of it, Holly had added "CFBR?" in a hue that made it fit in as if it had always been there. Her mouth hung open. "What the hell are you going to say if somebody like Spangler asks what it means?"

Holly laughed. "He already asked. I twisted his arm to come here and teach them how to take care of the orchid. Chester's in charge, but if he forgets, there are two others who know how. Pretty sweet, huh?"

"Very sweet, but what did you tell Spangler it meant?"

"That was easy," she said with a dismissive gesture. "It's our secret, but in everybody else's world, 'CFBR?' means 'Cattleya Finney, beautiful, right?'"

McCallister roared with laughter. "I cannot believe you!" Then, she suddenly went quiet. "Why, Hol? Why did you add it?"

"For you. If you *dare* go traipsing off into some unimaginable future again, this is all you are allowed to imagine. I figure when we're old, we'll get a room here. We'll only need a bedroom by then anyway; absolutely nothing else will matter. And I'll be such a successful artist that I'll be able to afford a whole parade of different Chinese restaurant delivery guys everyday, all day." She stopped to smile, and then she asserted, "This is *all* you get, babe. Do not look at anything else. We'll be together. Stop right there."

McCallister reached and squeezed her hand. "I love you so much!" she said, her heart full.

"Well, come on then. We have work to do." She took her arm and began heading back down the hall. "See, because when we're both old, you'll still be older than me. We need to be resourceful now while you're still limber." She laughed and then moved close to McCallister's ear. "If you can't stand without a walker, we'll need to know a variety of ways for you to be able to frisk me proper, copper."

Laughter carried them the rest of the way.

At the front door, they said their goodbyes to the residents. Holly reminded them that she would be back every other Tuesday. Then she threatened that if the orchid wasn't happy, there would be hell to pay. "Chester, you do your job! I mean it! Everybody else, do not cut him any slack just because he's such a looker. Otherwise, I will not let you guys kick my butt at cards ever again!"

156

McCallister and Holly strode back to the car. If it were at all possible, they would have felt closer. As it was, there were complete.

# About the Author

Rosalyn Wraight is the author of two other Detective Laura McCallister lesbian mysteries: *Woman Justice* and *Corpse Call*.

She is the author of the Lesbian Adventure Club series, which currently consists of ten titles: *Scavengers, Ledge Walkers, Savages, Loose Sleuths, Sisters, Leakers Ignited, Scraps, L-Word C-Word, Spiders,* and *Likely Suspects*. This ongoing series features Detective Laura McCallister, as well as various characters appearing in this title.

# On the Web

Author Website: LesbianWriter.com
Author Bookstore: LesbianAdventureClub.com

71332969R00105

Made in the USA
San Bernardino, CA
14 March 2018